for Jacob Smullyan

Contents

Preface

On December 10th, 1896 Alfred Jarry's play *Ubu Roi* premiered in Paris and closed the same night owing to the audience's violent hostility. It is now recognized as a major precursor of Dadaism, Surrealism, the Theatre of the Absurd and the Theatre of Cruelty. The play follows the exploits of the grotesque Père and Mère Ubu as they take and lose the throne of Poland (a partitioned nation that had lost its autonomy in 1830).

Ubu Roi has been the basis of many adaptations including an opera, a musical, films (big screen, TV and animated), modern day retellings and a cartoon strip. Marvin Cohen's play offers another twist whilst retaining the absurdity and cruelty of the original.

In March 2020, Marvin emailed: "I wrote [Booboo] because through James Laughlin of New Directions, I met the husband and wife authors, [Franciszka and Stefan] Themerson in London and read [Barbara Wright's translation for the Gaberbocchus Press], which inspired me with its sheer royal barbarity of being brutal and decisive to any opposition: pure powerful selfishness."

He more recently added this "psychological" explanation: "In the 1970s or 1980s I wrote this play after reading *Ubu Roi* by Jarry, (changing his "Ubu" to "Booboo" but keeping it in Poland), as a compensation for being poor, more than half deaf, and growing up in Brooklyn with poor parents . . . I envied my middle class contemporaries' privileges. I felt powerless and inferior to everyone. I had childishly daydreamed of having power over everyone, ruthlessly tyrannical, so I put myself in Ubu Roi's Booboo's shoes, and got imaginary literary revenge on the world."

—*Colin Myers*

Marvin Interviews Booboo, the Happy Dictator

I won't rest till I wreck the world.

What's your arch destructive method?

To systematically starve the poor and inject disease in them, a virtual universal plague that will also reduce my rich brethren to unprecedented poverty. I loot them of all their former wealth, including precious Rembrandts, to prove my cultural superiority and aesthetic sensibilities.

Aren't you going too far?

I'm merely being a loyal Fascist, serving my faith with religious fervor.

What's your ultimate aim?

To bring the world down to its collective defeated knees and simply take over as its Dictator, the Supreme King of all the local national rulers the globe over.

Isn't your exorbitant pride of malignant ambition setting you up to be overthrown by a cabal or confederacy of overturned rulers smarting for overdue revenge?

I'll be too well guarded. I'm not the incarnation of a second Julius Caesar, thus correcting classical history's weak precedent. I come prepared.

How did you get into the Fascism racket?

I studied Machiavelli and other political schemers who built or coached in empire building, to dynastic world-changing extents.

This all sounds too excessive.

I don't subscribe to the ancient Greek policy of moderation.

You're reckless.

Make a date to survey and admire my record once my World Domination is complete. Meanwhile, I don't trust you with my secrets. *(Suddenly, armed guards appear.)* Take this loser away. Subject him to torture convulsions, and take notes over his corpse for future strategic corrections down to the last boring details. I'm nothing, if not fussy.

Characters

Booboo

Madam Booboo

Captain Clarence

King Polski

His Queen

Palace Page

Court Psychiatrist

Common soldier ("Private Anonymous")

Others, sundry: Royal attendants, Polish soldiers,
Russian Czar and other European leaders,
Polish noblemen and citizenry,
the masses

Death

Time and *Place*: See title.

(*Quality* included there, also.)

Presentation: Literal. No symbols to be inferred.

(Note: Direction should be strict, throughout. Deviation from
the script would risk direct inaccuracy, and violate the play's
intention. The play has no intention.)

BOOBOO ROI

(The curtain opens, revealing Act One freshly narrated to the audience. The stage, as is sometimes said, is set.)

"So help me, but the world goes swimming by," admitted the pre-king of Poland on a nineteenth-century day in history.

"You sound like a fish instead of the mouse you are," nudged his wife, broad of beam, a plenitarian of vulgarity, whose antecedents still smelled of being fishmongers.

"What's your advice?" counseled the pre-king of Poland to his lady. "There's no lack of that from *you*," he added *offstage*, not intended for the boiled controversies of her ears; for instead of having earrings, her lobes hung the offenses she was always taking from the mouths of otherwise inoffensive people.

"Advice? What's the use of giving you what you don't take?" she urged, using psychology to make him take it.

"I *always* take your advice, even if I don't act on it," he replied on the defensive. Thus she had talked herself into advantage, which, true to herself, she seized upon.

(She *always* seized upon advantage; it was the only aggressive way to be practical and at the same time effective. She wasn't born to be a loser, Not she! Why otherwise would she have married—if not for personal ambition, and greed of increasing her rank in the known society of her day—this lout of a husband, who repulsively grew fatter every day in the disgusting way he had of putting on weight? He was already the pre-king of Poland, for she had her sights set on the throne which would make her queen for she was his wife. He had the confidence of the current king, and all that remained was for him to slaughter the king by surprise and then to have the king's heirs and families also slaughtered in kind, so as to ascend unopposed to the crownship of Poland's regal state. By *that* unkind act, *she* would be made queen, herself. For was she not already married to him? She would urge him to the deed, but would keep quiet about it except when speaking. And now she was speaking.)

"Booboo," (as she affectionately called her husband on familiar terms in their moments of ambitious intimacy which was always, for they aspired above their station in conjugal greed to outrank the others in social climbing for the spoils of their day such as they were, being "on the make" for what could be had), "Booboo, if you take my advice, I have advice to give you," she cooed, like Hera the wife of Zeus seducing great Zeus into sex bed to stall and lull his opposition to her plans for political gain; using the erotic game to gain her way or any other tactic that came to hand accessibly by the inspired route of direct expedience to administer to greed in the need and stroke of advantage when the hour to act is hot on the ripe daring of her timing to not let opportunity slide by. She was a sly one. Her fishmonger antecedents whose corpses still stunk had given her a legacy of cunning, she had inherited their instinct for cheating the fishermen of their hard-won wares, the toil of their labors, exploiting whatever the sea could yield to outbrazen Billingsgate market with fresh sea curses and salty cutthroatism.

She thrived under adverse competition; and now, while the chance was there, she'd induce her oaf of a husband, her dunce of a mate, Booboo, to slaughter the residing king and his heirs and kin forever, to usurp the bloody throne where side by side they'd sit with their ample backsides and not backslide, the king and queen by deed of violence, having illegally grabbed the throne as the only way to come by it, being not of royal lineage themselves nor next of line and so by their own hands and cruelly sticking their wits to the sticking point and plucking up their courage by dint of what they do in heroic dastardliness of foul intent by the brooding malice of their wills unflinching to be the stinking committers of so brutal an act that murder is too kind a word for it while evil bursts plunging into its dark and hideous self.

They'd be so stained with royal blood, that not even the multitudinous seas incarnadine could purge red away and whitewash out the filth that blots their moral record forever. It would tarnish their souls. But Poland's throne would compensate!

She'd urge him to it. If it were to be done at all, were best to be done now. Her sense of timing was quick to tell her that. Foul, foul. But get it over with. Do, do! And done, so it can't be helped.

Once done, is done. Then to get down to the results. And have for reward majesty complete.

(Act One, obscene two.)

(The would-be queen in future is assisting her mate to learn the blunt facts pearled within wisdom's worldly practicality:)

"Booboo, dear, you know the truth? We're not of royal descent. Nor are we loyal decent. We have to do it ourselves, to smite the reigning king and get the people on our side to herald what we've done as the great hour of *their* liberation. Yes, *that's* our motive: to free the populace! That's genius in me worthy of Machiavelli, to have put so noble an excuse on so ignoble an inexcusability in all the annals of filthy infamy perpetrated by a race never famous for their humanity though they come under the name of 'men', a word God gave them in an uninspired moment when nothing else came to hand and He had a deadline to meet . . . Dear, you're asleep! How I *do* wag on! Here, let me wake you."

(She clouts him over the head hard with a hard object, anything. It works, he wakes up.)

"Ah, that's better, you're awake. Caught you napping that time! What were your dreams like?"

"My head aches. It must mean I have a headache. Have you a pill or tablet for me to take?"

"Not pills and tablets, but pillars and tabernacles."

"What are you getting at, besides confusing me? What are you up to, my wife? What's inside your head? Don't hide it. I know there's something there. I'm your husband, so you must tell me. In marriage no secret must sunder man from wife. Tell, I beseech."

"I was thinking, my husband."

"Of course you were, my dear. You always do."

"What are you how? List your titles."

"I own a vast deal of ill-gotten property, taken by force, cheating principalities of their rightful domain. As an adventurer, I can lay claim to, among other spoils and booty, the Dukeship of Aragon, the Barony of Cambodia, and the Treachery of Talismania."

"The *Treachery*! What do you mean by that!"

"A derivation (or, in bastard terminology, 'corruption') of '*Treasury*.' I'm the chancellor of the exchequer, the keeper of the

3

coffers, the pursewarden, of that fair and noble land. As I'm their official Treasury Department, I help myself, hands over fists, to their taxes, revenues, and any other treasures they can afford. This keeps us rich and increases our wealth, by which our means expands, by which we can lay our hands on the prize I covet, which is Poland's promised land, of which I've designated myself *pre-king*, in honor of China's capital, *Peking*."

"You're *peeking* East."

"Of what are you speaking?"

"You're piquing me."

"I'm at my peak. I eke East to Orient myself to what by Occident I'm about to take: that crushed, crucified, persecuted plot of history, Poland, squeezed between two brutes of countries that overrun it like the Huns and barbarians that they are: the Russian bear and the German bar-bear(ian). Poland has been drained so often by such disparate pincers, that it's meet and fit I myself should help myself to whatever is left. I'll leave the culture alone, and take the gold."

(Admiringly;) "Spoken like a true man worthy of being *my* husband. I *love* your ideals, they're so noble. I shall be proud to share them with you. Our ideals are as good as gold. That's logical, for they *are* gold. What more do we want? Just gold, plain gold. It'll have to do, it'll have to be good enough for us. That's all we want, just that. But *lots* of it! The trick is to get it by the *quantity*. *That's* the challenge. As a husband-wife team, we're a bit mercenary, and out for all we can get. Why not? We don't like art, we like gold. We have to compensate for our lack of culture. The more gold we acquire, the less inferior we'll feel culturally, socially, and otherwise. Gold is our nice, precise means of self-preservation. I love as much of it as possible. The more gold we have, the less *pretentious* we have to be. Why should we have middle-class pretentiousness, when we can get upper-class where-with-all? I want aristocratic blood to be dripping in my veins. No, that's not enough. *Royal* blood, at least. We have to fight for it, for we're not born with it. It's ours for us to take, by force, to make up for not having it at the start. The more gold we have, the more we can *buy* it. We need retainers, an army

4

to protect us, our devoted followers, and we have to support them. It takes *gold*; even the edge of guilt can be gilt-edged, and eased off. We'll make off with all the products and profits of guilds, by gilding our robbery on our glittering shield that wards off any leaden accusation! What a golden path, to our nation's ruin!"

"You're shining, dear! Coin on!"

"Only *golden* means will do; dross is for lower stakes. We must plunder the state. Where there's a will, there's a mint. Avarice is the limit. Yet necessity craves more. Even *plenty* is insufficient, if the quantity is modest. *Gain* must be our increase. Is that plain?"

"You whisper 'power' between the lines. You talk most temptingly, Madam. Your point is very bright indeed."

"Let's grab all we can. No use stinting, we need all we can get. Our ambition is abnormally high: in fact illegal. Gold then is the more needed. It'll cost us, plenty, to get what we want, but once we get there, we'll begin to get paid back, and get a good old royal profit. We'll bleed every Polish peasant and burgher alike of everything they can muster by tax. The people will suffer, for our benefit. We don't mean to go into the monarchy business (*getting* there is the thing—aye, there's the rub) for the charity of it, except as the charity has us as beneficiaries, exclusively, to funnel all the wealth into our palatial household. Why be benevolent despots, when we can rule heavy-fisted and get away with whatever we want by divine right of our rightful monarchies which shall be the might to acquire goods endlessly at everyone else's expense and not stop? My eye glitters. Our prospects turn all gold."

(Her speech ended, she looks for approval to her husband, with a firm and searching glance. He dares not withhold it, but breaks out into frank admiration, with a childish eagerness in his impulsive, piggish applause. This he soon checks, to attain the grave dignity of irony and restraint, in sophisticated understatement in keeping with the crowned role he hopes legitimately to soon affect in the wrested power to be.)

"I have an intelligent wife. When she speaks, I listen. When I listen, I agree. Am I not being agreeable?"

"Ah, let me hug you, my beast! We were meant for each other! Ours was a marriage made in . . ."

(They repress the word which rhymes with "bell," and sink into an obese embrace. The curtain decorously comes down, to modestly hide their shame from the appalled audience in whom morality is urgent for all the immorality heard contemplated, brash plans afoot horrid but purposed. The curtain again rises on:)

(Act Eight. For we've skipped ahead, ruthlessly deleting anything irrelevant to this well-made play built on classical models.)

Booboo and his wife have summoned Clarence, the Captain of the Dragoon Guards, an elegant young officer sumptuous and dashing in his uniform of supreme military insolence. He bristles with suave poise, an honors graduate from the leading military academy, released to a brilliant career. He bends over the blunt couple, with his sabre sword leaping gleamingly from its restraining holster with bloody eagerness for its savage commission. "At your service," he intones to his pair of rotund employers, whom he will use for personal advancement to the head of the renegade army when such an army occasions to get itself formed as the festivities are bound to dictate with the coup d'état soon to be braved by Booboo who doesn't want it bungled or his head will be cut off instead of the crown placed thereon. Much depends, therefore. Clarence is indispensable. He bends an ear, as the hot plot is proposed.

"You must help us out, good Clarence. He'll make it worth your while. We'll charge you to gather and lead an army in support of our sudden overthrow of the kindhearted, too trusting current king of the realm, Polski, whose crown shall change heads and is meant to cap my hour of glory, aided in full force by you, Clarence, and your charges, whom I handsomely commission to do battle in fury and heroic valor when most it counts to force present royalty out and thrust me in, Booboo, along with my gracious wife. King Polski shall be overthrone, and on that toppled place *I'll* roost, to rule and crow. You'll be my minister, Clarence, as part of your fee. You'll be the brag of my new-formed court, its leading courtier. Unblemished aristocratic heiresses will vie for your disdainful favors and the contempt of your flashing eye. Fashion will be centered on you. *Our* new royal persons are fat and ugly. *You* will cut a brilliant figure, and turn all heads romantically. Join us, Clarence."

"What's in it for me *now*?" the swaggerer asks.

"Captain, we cross your palm with these dozen ducats, these high-currency ingots, and here, these usury-spawned shekels from the lower confines of our shady purse. These will do you for the hence, as pincushions for your petty cash expenses in molding a

7

mighty army from the ranks of the mouldering royal one. Without you, Captain, our conspiracy isn't worth a groat. Our impending misadventure is calculated exactly to your contribution, and to my pluck, and to my wife's stratagems by guile of her cunning won by her fishmongering ancestry in vile deceptions played on empty-bellied fishermen in low wharfs where awful bait lured only bony fish and their paltry sea relatives from skimpy caverns in oceanic waste. Clarence, we opulently promise you real gold when our deed succeeds to demote Polski into history as a former king, cutting off his life at a single slice from my itching sword. We'll pay you off to such a tune that the song sings itself. It'll strum your strings to a rhapsody of pelf and wealth, ill-begotten gains to sugar your lyrical harp that your knee shall dandy while maidens melt like candy for any warrior's embrace you'll bear them from your proud and proven arms. The rewarding soldier's life will keep you fornicating all the night once the throne is ours. Give me your shaking hand to clinch this deal, and may this arrange our terms to put the conspiracy afoot on steady gait on the dirt road of our pact leading to the plush carpet and palace revels, high debauchery, privileged decadence, degenerate luxury, the crown extravagances and the wasting festivities that were ancient indulgences topped by us in the celebrant triumph of evil that's stolen a kingdom from a king's trust.

"Poor Polski, I'm his chief mourner already, his fall from fortune is great, while our rise is vile, but such is a law of life, in its mischief-worn plot. The depraved succeed. The noble are sacrificed. Dignity is debased in currency. False rank deposes genuine worth. All over Europe, the monarchy lights are going out. The high Viennese emperor is soon ousted, the latest I've heard. The fashion is the democratic coup. It's the dawn of liberalism, I'm afraid. Such ideals are not mine. They're mine to *capitalize* on, though. Right, my wife? Do we heed beckoning opportunity, dear? Or do our scruples deafen it?"

"Great Booboo, scruples are petty. Qualms do harm. Better to rule a state, than to regret it. Poland is ripe-taken. It's *asking* for us to plunder. *Not* to is a blunder. Nothing need detain us, as we've weaned our consciences away from the milk of guilt. Better for us the bold wine of the committer too drunk to repent. We'll topple, well, Polski's tower. Snug in our fist purrs all meek Poland, kissing our power. I'm game! I'm game! The royal hunt is on!"

(She whoops, with bright joy flushing her anticipation. Captain Clarence smirks, then answers, at this rowdy, uncouth demonstration. He's too much the dandy to like open conduct where frankness shows. Then he closes his sneer, politic, civil, urbane, meekfeigning. He bows haughtily, and takes his leave, like a practiced courtier already, perfumed with bland stale practice to the jaded fripperies.) "Good day, pre-king Booboo. And you too, Mistress Madam Booboo, the queen soon to be. I've got to go out and train my army. First I've got to enlist them in our cause. I'll pretend we're loyal, of course. The stress of danger is met nicely by deceit when pressed at a delicate point. My diplomacy will come in handy here. I'm esteemed in pride by virtue of my vice, for evil is good these days, as the odor of corruption infests the court and causes the windows to be flung open even in our Polish February with the snow having migrated across the border from Russia's drifting surplus. Lord Booboo and Lady, good day. My cape flies away, and I before. Our plot thickens. May its ways prosper."

(Off romps Clarence, then. By the way, is Booboo a sure Pole; if not, what is he doing here? Same for *Mrs* Booboo. She stems from Billingsgate market, which is by the London Thames. They're adventurers both, chancing Polish luck. Their enemy feet lord it on unsuspecting Polish soil, as stoutly their shadows grow to personify national peril. They look funny, but they're dangerous. The king is too trusting. It's to be his tragic flaw, when all comes true being brooded now. The lurking foulness ponders heavy business ahead.)

(Next Scene; with its number lost count of in the heaviness of the thick and grimy plot that pollutes clarity to undo a king and install gross Booboo instead and his fusty wife, broad-bottomed both, on the seat of splendor which Polski and his queen will see overthrown in their pre-death flash of final illumination before darkness conquers all. This scene shows Booboo and his wife fooling around, feeling for frisky prank in the frolic of amusement before they assume their grim burden. They're in the garden of their rented mansion, sipping tea from a jigger. Picture it? Good. From Booboo's puffy face these words burst forth, bold fronts by which his mounting internal anxiety and sop-cowardly misgivings are bravado-disguised in insolent exulting over the fate to befall the eminence of his titled victim confidently proclaimed with blithe tomfoolery under the garden awning before a snow-blanched scene to keep spring under a burden of delay on sluggish underfoot seasonal dullness, the lull before the explosive personal revolution that Booboo will wreck upon kindly Polski's poll when insubordination grows its excess doom to ruin the honor vested in authority and mock all codes of justice in the famed realm of Poland:)

"My pre-queen, if you're wise, then why is so much snow in our garden?"

"To give testimony to it having snowed, my lord."

"Not a bad answer. Lacking in warmth, though. I think, now, of our friend, King Polski, and his royal consort. His reign has short to live, in my will's calendar. He trusts us, he likes us; we'll thrust him where his trust lodges, in his blood-blossoming breast, under his armor plate, and his casual Majesty shall find too late his trust was ill reposed. I wonder the size of his head. Would his crown fit me? Wife, I beg you for your millinery opinion. Am I too thick to wear his crown? Or will my ugly deed swell my head bloater than a pig's bladder? I want to wear the kingdom in dignity. Will Poland sit well on me, in its jewelled splendor? Or will not gold, but guilt, crush me in my head of state? I wish to wear my stolen hat in style. Does my style suit it? Or will it betray my unbecomingness to wear it? Answer, fat mate. Or I'll trounce you, you sack of fish."

"Your address is slighting. Cut out the invective. My temper is wrath-riled on slow provocation, and I'll counter-insult you out of countenance to do you in before, oaf, you do our high-placed victim in. Ambition is puffing in your head with the swollen consistency of a balloon sculpted in the round in permanent leather to outweather any puncture at the point of a pin. You hog's-girth, you mouse-morality, you fish-brain, you arrogant stick of nothing glutted round with pulp of protective fat! I loathe you, but love what you're to be, with I the bridal queen when the present one has died. Hasten that day! Historically dark it shall be. But sun-bright, in my personal life! Booboo, I'm glad I married you. Not knowing in my stars that it was to be *Poland* I married! For I'm English-born, on the Thames. Nor are you, Booboo, a Pole either. Yet we're very much here, we're here more here, than any born native of it. We've come to reign, to rule! Our passports are thereby valid. Foreigners though we be, yet all Poland is soiled to us. On *its* soil, this state goes soiled, as we pilfer all its yield of farm or town, all goods boiled down into our gold. Not bad. We've come far. We'll stay, I think. It likes me, here."

(The next Act is in the same place. The Act has advanced, but the Scene stays still. Progress is more in time than in place, at least here.)

(The pre-king and the pre-queen, villains both by intention and confession, are seen in their chamber garden adjoining the deer park grounds that give access to the royal palace itself, misty with grandeur, goal of assassins. Booboo, very fat, is chewing on a chicken leg while standing up plotting the overthrow of the state. A change of heart comes upon him, and he weakens.)

"My darling wife, my resolve is weakened because I'm a coward and afraid that if we don't succeed we'll be punished through execution and hung and drawn and quartered as traitors against the king. My fear is so strong that it's being rationalized by delusions of tender, compassionate mercy for our beloved king. He's such a nice man that he oughtn't die. We're *worse* people, we have no right to kill him, for he's better than us. And besides, he would kill us if our attempt failed. That's what I'm *really* driving at. I have a rush of prudence to circumvent my headstrong rashness. In short, I'm afraid."

"Be undaunted, my true love. Let me rouse you to courage, and encourage you to rise to the destiny we can make if we will it. Be not lily-livered, nor soft-blooded, when iron resolve must steel your heart to that eunuch-breeder, doubt. Be great, Booboo. Or I'll kill you."

"I'm glad we have no children. But if we did, only the *man*-child could pipe from your breast your potent brew of nursing blood, as you give suck to your whelp, for your ferocious pup would be sopped by no milk from your mammaries, nay, no milk of human kindness would have the tenderness to drop from your pumps; but the oil of vampires, or the poisoned urine of hate, or the snake's sperm, or other hideous potions strictly alcoholic in content giving drunken license to insane criminal tendencies, regalmania, the psychotic longing for secular Highness, the hysteria of a craving beyond all pomp. No cream would issue from your dugs, but the boiling beverage of the infernal pot spiked with the devil's armpit sweat that causes aphrodisia of crown perversion and leaks the scum of monarch's surgical pus from the open vanity wound. You're a proud woman. You *deserve* to be my wife."

"I liked the *ending* of your speech, though not pleased till then. Clarence has gone to alert the retinue of our armed followers upon the scheme we intend. How's King Polski himself? Not sick, I hope."

"You need not feel too concerned that His Majesty wears ill health. For his good health would then give itself healthily to his bloody demise. My *sword* will do it, I think. It has a sharp blade. The thin skin of the king will be easily sliced. It's but child's play. Then *I* succeed, to the fallen crown, when Clarence brings his aid in, an army strong. Our slaughter must include the queen, and all royal relatives or dim family connections with even a *faint* natural claim to what *we* take by illegitimate means. We'll put in our unnatural bid, which Clarence's mighty aggregate shall enforce in full, its endorsing throng loyal to our disloyalty. Ours will be the day, and fate our plaything. Then we must woo public opinion. A few strategic lies will do the trick. Propaganda is a refined art. I've hired some publicity experts. They'll create popular approval of our hideous crime. We'll be called liberators. It'll be said Polski was a tyrant. His rebuttal is sealed up in death. We'll be lauded, as saviours, patriots supreme. Poland will lay itself at our feet. We'll rub the boot in, and smooth its collective face, stomp its body politic. But later, not yet. First for the king's death. That's big enough, and done under critical difficulty unless we allay all suspicion from his ruling body of advisers and his queen of clairvoyant paranoia. Cassandra-like, let her be doom's unheeded prophet, and her warning ridiculed. Polski is a trusting type. That's our key to the throne. Up we thrust. And down the blade. Off the king's neck, or his breast shall take it bare. Brutal, but neat. We shall execute. No cringing to betray us. Bold and swift, let's be. To prise away Majesty. And die in it, for Kingdom Come."

"When age is ripe, not soon. I intend to be an elderly queen."

"But *lean* people live old. The fat are afflicted, and lose hold."

"Kings prove exceptions. They *set* the rule, not obey."

"Thank you, madam, for affirming us. Top public relations and advertising personnel are planning a campaign to vindicate our moral deed; as our apologists they'll warm our reception into the hospitable Polish citizen who knows only what he reads. We'll take over the press, and release lying bulletins and editorial praising to affirm the overthrow as an act long overdue to replace concealed bad with belated good. Ours is a reform regime, the broadcast will go. The Poles will show gratitude where it hurts, by the belt of taxes. Half all incomes will be ours. We'll promote poverty by stealth, in sneaky ruse, while proclaiming the good we do. Hypocrisy is a coarse method, but true. It much accords by us, our nature mirrored by it. The future stands blueprinted. Let's implement it, and soon. My Lady, summon Clarence in. He's our smooth spokesmen, impressing slyly in representing what by modesty we can't be direct about. Too much exposure bodes no good, for our hide. Let *Clarence* be seen, give *him* the fame. No worthier proxy have we. His slime is oily to persuade. Let's *us* keep to the shade. We give out a gross appearance. *His* elegance wins hearts. Ours gives revulsions. Statesmanship is the art of what *seems*. *Seeming* is our trick. What *is*, is dirty. But *appearance* cleans it up: causes dust to shine and grime to thrill in virtue's radiance from a seeming heaven. We *must* be clever: it's political to be.

"What's *hide*ous, shall be hid. We shall kid these Polish kids. Undetected, convincing. Our porch shall reek virtue, in its seen edifice. Our back-room shall store up filth, but we won't leak it. What's *seen* is pure. That's what the public shall know, being fed. What *is*, is *our* business. Best it remain private. It's our concealed sin. Sealed off from our name. Our best name is presented forward; all rot withheld. This is the art of publicity. It sells products: ourselves. We get a good institutional brand name. It shall do in the stead of what's revolting but true. The public be led. Blindly led, by our own cunning sights. *Our* sights to be led by the lights of self-interest, to which all is subordinate including every Polish fool who lives. Even Clarence, should his usefulness fade, is a fit sacrifice to our needs. We come first. Nothing else is second. The only number is ourselves. Only one."

"But we're both fat, and there are *two* of us."

"Two make one, in our case. Are we not married?"

"That we are, and by legal bond."

"We're one, then. Let's serve us."

"*Us?* But all you do is please your*self.* How do *I* get in, on goods and spoils left over, once your greed hogs it all?"

"Serving myself, is to be *continually* at your service. By my selfishness, you'll make history's most gratified queen; your extremest greed shall seem modest: we'll so contrive things, that blessings fall due in our reward in nature's honest measure. Our very extravagance will seem self-effacing. Does that suit you, madam? If you're pleased, curve your lips to a smile."

(Mrs Booboo seems adoringly thrilled.) "Booboo, I can kiss you now."

"Do so. Or I'll take a mistress when King."

"You're repulsive. Women of court would only fancy Clarence."

"The king, though fat, gets what he wants. He commands an eminent position. People fawn and obey him. He knows but subjects. Women, too, are subjects."

"Should you take a mistress, I'll take a lover. *Clarence* would be nice. I'll bid him into my bed. He can't refuse."

"You're the grossest queen ever. But you're dreaming. Elegant Clarence would never want you. The beauty you lack would fill a world. And if he *anyway* obeys, I'll simply have him murdered. For I'm king."

"Then I'll have *you* murdered. For I'm queen."

"Such idle talk!"

"Poison would do it. I'd pour it into your soup, having bribed our imperial cook. Then what's cooked is your goose. Then I'll have whom I choose, unlike Victoria, who remained a chaste widow and kept Britain mourning. *I'm* British, you know."

"Yes. From fishy waters."

"Stop dragging that in. Wash out what's in your net. You hooked worm!"

"Stop, grossness! We're not royal yet. Tomorrow's the day. All is set."

"You wanted Clarence summoned. Shall I call?"

"At once, my prize. We've got to get our signals straight, in timing to the King's demise. All the King's followers get slaughtered, the whole royal family of pretenders, heirs, and hangers-on. We want Poland *freshly* ours. Hence, the purge."

(Thus they're resolved. A few more Acts and Scenes go by. Finally we hit upon the next one. It'll be unusual, for it begins where the Booboos reside ((same as where we left off)), and switches, in mid-scene, to a new scene, which is the royal bedchamber, where the Queen broods and King Polski sleeps. The Queen will be seen as profoundly worried, once the Scene switches over there. This whole Act with its split-in-two Scene is done without dialogue, but rather with the omniscient narrator's chorus-like descriptive critical moral commentary, as from above without its being dramatically enacted by the characters. The plot is brewing, with Mr and Mrs Booboo and Clarence being the bad people, and with the King and Queen of Poland ((doomed, alas)) being the good ones. Bad has the aggressive momentum on its side, and so is apt to carry the day; Good is unsuspecting in the King's case, and but impotently defensive in the Queen's. Bad decidedly has the edge. This has pessimistic implications on the moral scale, on justice and retribution. A metaphysical sermon will be delivered at the Act-Scene's end on the cosmic fate of man in his sad state. A sweeping survey of history in time and place will be seen swiftly in flight, but right now, summoned Clarence comes in to blend in to the conspiracy afoot of which the Booboos are author-villains, that coarse and repugnant couple whose foulness permeates the whole play and stinks out the atmosphere. We have to put up with them. They're central to the plot. They concoct evil, and Clarence joins in. willingly. Even to outdo them. He has the good taste to detest them. As they are detestable, Clarence demonstrates a realistic trait. But curses are on him. His own evil stinks too. Only the Royal Couple are good. Good being ineffectual and mild; evil forceful, to ply its way. Poland is the world. It will have to suffer, as immorality's rife victim. Gullible innocence makes easy prey. Wickedness is drawn to it. This is Darwin's world, but it's not his fault. He only found it to be. Blame the Booboos and young Clarence. They act out the bad. But the bad pre-existed them; and will go on after. They only illustrate: they didn't create. It's a sorry state. But there it is: the world's way. We just comment on this, and watch it be. Life is tragic in society. All the cultures of civilization—witness this nineteenth-century Polish version—weigh bad over good in the way things come out to be. This is a gloomy view. But not inaccurate, no?)

Clarence enters, with military bearing, and surly officer insolence, showing faint distaste. He considers Booboo and wife vulgar, of plebeian stock, and foreigners to boot. He'd boot them, too. He plans to overthrow them, once they become king and queen. They're being used as pawns: by him who's *their* pawn. The power intrigues at court are already sprung from complex germs. First to rid the palace of Polski, and all his train. That's the theme of this interview, held in whispering secret. They rehearse their roles and what's each to do. Thoroughness is a precautionary cover. Nothing can be afforded to go wrong. There's a mortal penalty attached to failure. The life-force detests that: thus, determination is on success. The plot is fool-proof. Nothing left to chance, all flaws eliminated, all links tightened, the whole a masterpiece. A conspirators' dream, if it comes off. The scheming goes on all night, in a candle-lit room. The candle lights two fat faces and one haughty one. All three hearts brood evil alike. But Clarence looks ahead, in future device. He'll contrive his two colleagues dead, once their fellow-conspiracy works. It's his own private *counter-conspiracy*. On the Booboos' parts they, but more vaguely in an imprecise stage, brood the end of Clarence, once his use to them has been served. Three knavish criminals are at work. Oh how they misrepresent earth! And beautiful Poland's rape!: it doesn't touch them *pathetically*, but in earnest: to *promote* such rape, bring it soon about. It's all for tomorrow: tomorrow is the First of March. The candle flickers. Midnight screeches in. Wolves howl, from distant woods. Witches go about on invisible broomsticks. Evil is loose. All the omens conspire. The moon runs bloody. Lions are romping, in from Africa. Reality turns hallucinatory. Madmen are about, in raving packs. They mutter accurate prophecies. The scene turns to the King's palace. Polski slumbers in innocence. The Queen is wild awake. She must warn him. She senses only trouble. Tomorrow there's a military review. All the forces will be on show, to muster arms. There'll be elaborate drills; even mock warfare. The Russian and German ambassadors will attend: every national foe, and also friend. Polski will preside. Clarence will maneuver the troops. Booboo will be there, and his Madam. What is he up to? The Queen is highly suspicious. She has grave intuition. It bespeaks uncanny accuracy. An assassination plot is afoot! She in her crystal ball has detected it! How to warn Polski, though? He won't heed! His serenity is royal indeed. There's been peace in the realm. He hasn't learned to suspect. She's got to allay his lack of suspicion. How!? He'd mock her, only; say she was given to "seeing things". So noble and unimaginative is he: a baby, an innocent! See him, in his sleep! He could be dead, before day is over! Disarmed, disarming, is he. But he has an unknown enemy. The Queen suspects Booboo: there's an evil stuck in his grossness. And *Lady* Booboo is almost worse! Oh, this night will never end. She must wait, wait. Till past dawn. Then will the King wake. He'll call for breakfast. She'd *try* to tell him, *try*! Oh believe, King! Believe, or you die! The Queen prays. At the foot of the bed. On both her knees. She's parallel to the King's head. "God, Poland is asleep. Guard it well. But Poland could be dead. *Alarm* my husband to this, please! Plant in him a doubt of Booboo. Only doubt and vigilance can save the state. Else, it's *evil's* reign. And death of all good things!"

She swooned, after praying this. Her mouthful was heard, by God. But God that early morning, happened to be Russian. It purposed Him well, then, for Poland to incur trouble. It could be ruined internally: thanks to Booboo's agency. Then the Russian active forces could step in: they'd "rescue" the raped maiden. By "rescue," "confiscate." To enlarge the Bear's bold estate. Devils Russian in, where fools fear to tread. Poland is going under! God wills it! And what God wants, God gets. Booboo's in His commission, unknowingly. Small evils are outdone by vaster ones. The large fish devours the small; then gets devoured by a larger one. Poland ravished by Booboo? Then Russia "saves" it? "Protects" it? And by "protect," to "possess." Oh dark laws! Who's the world's architect? The Devil is; and God's his chief engineer, to put the machinery to effect. Then evil rules? Who's good's exponent? Where's the advocate of heaven's own counterplan? Advocate and plan were burned: hell raised its fire, to smoke out anything above. We're in darkness. The world is Booboo's. Very nature assists him. Poland's Queen goes back into bed: alongside her doomed and sweet Polski. She'll recite by rote her warning, after the pale crack of morning. Polski is a good man; he assumes goodness in others. His stature is above suspecting Booboo. Too high above. High enough, for *tragedy* to accompany the fall. For tragedy can keep gravity company in a grievous descent. At gravity's bottom, a grave waits. There for tragic Polski to reside. Booboo to dance on top of it. The winner's wife too, lightly for her bulk; over the losing Queen, supine. The divine trodden; the base on top. But the base to be devoured: Clarence to take over. Then Clarence felled; and political cannibalism continues. Nations in their feast of strife. Brute might remains to reason up the rational appeal of its apology; having eliminated the rest. Into the face of time. On generational flight. Dynasties razed. But the tradition is perpetuated. Democracies take their place. And do also the same. Can eternity put a stop to this? God only knows. The race renews itself, on the human-faced earth. The Booboos have no children. But *other* Booboos do.

(Now we go to the next Scene, which belongs to a still further Act. It's morning on March First, the King woke up and had his customary breakfast and went to the bathroom. Now he joins his wife in the throne room. They sit on adjoining thrones, with their crowns on. The Queen will plead that he beware. He'll mock her warning. He'll mock what could save his life; he lacks the imagination to conceive evil. He regards Booboo as his friend! He's deficient in foresight. Fatally so, in all likelihood. The wheels turn; in motion is the arch machinery. To devour the royal pair? Without it being averted? Blind to his welfare, there's no evil to see, for the King. So he's unaware. He's happy now. What will he be tonight? He has no dread. The Queen speaks. He heeds not. To his loss? Oh, let's see!)

"Look, dear, you've got to listen to me. I have this awful hunch. I'm not just speaking through an idle crown. I'm warning in *earnest*! *Regard* it, please."

"You're silly and nervous. You love me so hysterically you're afraid of losing me. There's nothing to *fear*. Except, maybe, fear itself. I'm not being brave: merely calm."

"Darling, do me this favor: do *not* attend the military parade of this afternoon, and the gallant maneuvers conducted under young Clarence's rather dashing leadership, who has turned the heads of the court ladies with his arrogant ways that present evil in a charming guise. There's a real danger. It's not in my head. If you attend, if you preside, I predict what's too horrible to think of, I've got to choke back my scream. Booboo with his sword will cut you through, and by that stroke divorce the soul I love from my man's body. It's all so true: so stay home, dear. Make yourself cosy. Balzac's latest novel has arrived, you can read it by the fireplace, on this snow-blanched first day of March; and our servants will have tempting morsels of food for you, to nibble on after lunch despite the advice of our dietician and hygiene master who wishes us to slim up to avoid looking as grotesque as Booboo and his frightful wife. Oh, there's our page. Page, what do you want?"

(Page, to King:) "Your Highness, a man to see you. It's Lord Booboo. Shall I announce him?"

(King:) "Yes, page, do so. Bid my friend in." (Page exits. To Queen:) "He's harmless, you'll see. He loves us. His loyalty stands stout. I won't malign him with doubt. You're absurd, dear Queen. It's weak of you to suspect him. Such paranoia deserves treatment by our royal psychiatrist. Don't fail to make an appointment to have your fears checked. Latent anxiety will be indicated, a close mental examination will reveal. He'll have to alter your diet, and prescribe some cures, such as taking a hot bath to alleviate horrid imaginings. Your diseased brain must get proper rest and remedy, for you go on in your refrain how Booboo means harm. Why, there he is!" (Booboo has entered.) "Welcome, loyal friend! No, don't bow nor bend. Why stoop to ceremony, here? Your courtesy is in your *heart*. You offend me by obsequious gesture that demeans your ample person. Don't betray my love with cold formal mannerism. Be cordially familiar, I beg. You and I, we're one, are we not?"

(Booboo's voice cunningly dissembles intimate friendship but humble loyalty:) "Your Majesty is but too flattering, or should in equality I call you by your Christian 'Polski'? Would that be too intimate?"

"It's my wish, Booboo. To you I'm Polski; to others, King."

(Queen:) "Please, dear, don't trust Booboo. You can't see what I can see. He means the end of you. His eye sees you dead, already."

(King, to Queen:) "I'm furiously annoyed with you, my dear. How dare you accuse my friend here! His love for me rivals mine for him. You offend his innocence, by imputing evil intentions to his loyal heart. I bid you silence in his presence." (To Booboo:) "Forgive her outburst, please. She has demented delusions these days. She suspects a plot! In paranoia she's conjured a conspiracy! Can you imagine that! Gentle Booboo, forgive her. She raves."

(Booboo:) "She needs some mental therapy. Is she being treated psychiatrically?"

"How compassionate and kind of you, Booboo, to recognize her ill." (Rings for Page. Page enters.)

(Page:) "Yes, your Majesty."

(King:) "Summon the psychiatrist, tell him hurry, the Queen's condition is an emergency, she needs help and calm nerves."

(Page runs off to do as told.)

(Queen, to King:) "I'm angry. *You*'re insane: you'll die by it, I'm afraid. I'm *sane*, I insist: and I, too, must die for it. Because *you* can't *see*. See Booboo?" (Points to Booboo.) "He's only after killing you; then me, and all. He wants your crown, your throne. He's a greedy man! See that?"

(The King rises. The psychiatrist comes running in. King, to psychiatrist:) "Seize her at once, she's raving, take her away, make an informal immediate appointment, she's possessed by some foul spirit, some evil-obsessed sprite, and you've get to exorcise her of it. She's plain nuts, I'm afraid. Cure her, or be fired and replaced. I can hire the Austrian Freud, or the Swiss Jung, they're both top men in their field, to root out the diseased thought in my afflicted wife, with their tenacious ministrations to raze from sight such terrors in her sight that block her in to feeble blindness to outer things the while there rage imaginary demons to curse her sight against simple sanity's light, such as upon kind Booboo she dares to thrust the unfounded killer's motivation to turn crown-assassin! Better charge an angel with designs on the holy life of Jesus strung up on an old cross! It's not to be borne, such madness!"

(Psychiatrist:) "I'll mend her at once, Your Majesty, and return her sane to you if any sanity remains in her poor addled head that confuses Booboo with malice on your life at peril to the alleged threat he poses by invention of the Queen's mind now shipwrecked on distraction's sandy beach in private dungeons of the self where worlds shrink alarmed by an idea that grows to monster enlargement independent of external reference to what actually is going on in actual rational reality's state of truthful being. I'll give her illumination, Sir, by the *sun*, not by her candle's personal assumption of Booboo's looming gross in danger's malevolency by dragging you out of Poland into Death where your crown goes unrecognized for the vital power it commands here. I'll straighten her out, Sir. My methods apply to this case to perfection. She has Booboo-on-the-brain, but I'll clean her of that image which does unjust insult to the true Booboo now present. I'll restore reality to her, from which her split is opening, removing her to a far shore. I'll bring her back, Sir, as herself. In good shape, bathed anew in the spa or well or springs of pure, transformative, fluid, and open reality. She'll be like new, Sir. Or if not, she was incurable."

(King, to Booboo:) "My apologies, Booboo. Forgive her just now. She's sundered from the real, but we hope to patch it up. Otherwise I personally shall be quits of her. If she divorces reality, and *I*'m part of reality, then she shall also divorce me, and I'll go and find a new queen among the maidens of my kingdom who boast by pedigree enough nobility of blood and by good fortune enough beauty of their persons." (Dreamingly:) "That could be a welcome change, lecherously."

(Psychiatrist seizes the struggling Queen and abducts her from the throne room as King sternly approves.)

(King sighs in relief, his tense tone dissolves in relaxing warmth. Gentle doses of noble generosity now pour in larger waves from his open, magnanimous heart.) "Well, Booboo, at last some peace. My wife has vacated her throne. It's comfortable up there, beside me. Step on the platform and take her place, dear Booboo."

"Polski, I'd rather sit where *you* are. Could *you* take *her* throne, and I yours?"

"Certainly. Glad to oblige the whim of a friend." (King shifts over to Queen's throne. Booboo seats himself on *King's* throne.) "Are you satisfied, dear subject?"

"Not yet, gracious Polski. One thing remains to make my pleasure complete."

"Mention it, and I'll confer the favor."

"Your crown: may I try it on?"

"Naturally. Here." (Doffs his crown, presents it to Booboo. Booboo takes it and puts it on.)

"Ouch, it hurts, being so heavy. Didn't it discomfort you, wearing it so regularly? Or did your wearied head learn insensitivity to this valued physical pressure?"

"I got used to it. In truth, I wear my crown lightly.'

"Not, however, now."

"No. *You* have it, now."

"And mean, I'm afraid, to keep it."

"You mean to delay returning it? Wear it as long as you like. It's only in play."

"You're generous, King. Your generosity shall die!"

"What strange words! What mean they, Booboo?"

(Booboo glances at his wristwatch, then takes out a whistle and blows it. Clarence comes rushing in at the head of a small, mobile battalion, ready at arms upon the order to fire on the notice of an instant, by pre-arranged signal; thus contradicting in improvisational option the original plan of saving the assassination for the military parade festivities later in the day. Opportunity has announced itself precociously, so let the preconceived scheme go hang, as that blueprint now turns obsolete, which the Queen had forecast.

Thus the Queen's prophecy is inaccurate, in small detail of the *timing* of the killing. Essentially, she's turned out right, in the wrongdoing itself. She's not there to say "I told you so," having been spirited away by the promptly obedient psychiatrist as the King had furiously commanded. The Queen had been deficient in *courtesy*. That's fatal, in *court*. Booboo had been an honored guest. The chivalrous King sided with him in protection against his mate's scandalously ill-bred implications. The King's protection, extreme hospitality, had warmed Booboo well. He had been accorded the privilege, rarely requested, of wearing for fun the King's own crown and sitting on his own private throne. Will Booboo abuse the King's generous concessions? Most probably, yes. Booboo is indelicate, in returning small tokens of courtesy. He rivals his wife as a boor.

Meanwhile, here's Clarence having arrived with armed followers. This crowds the throne room up, what will take place, summarily? Nothing drastic, we hope. No ruinous catastrophe for Poland, that annihilates justice at a single bound. No, Booboo and Clarence are there only for *fun*, we hope. Or else the King's life is not safe. What will young Clarence say?)

(Clarence:) "The King has no attendants whatever, for his protection! How imprudent of him!"

(King, to Clarence:) "Why, Clarence! How pleased I am to see you! But why have you brought all these troops in here? There's no trouble for them to defend against!"

(Clarence:) "Not to defend, Majesty, but *offend*."

(King, jocularly:) "Clarence, how quaint! You're in very witty form today. Most amusing."

(Booboo:) "The King is laughing at our 'joke'. It's funny to him. That's a good time to catch him, while he's doubled over on *her* throne in a paroxysm of merry mirth. Unsuspecting to the end! Unguarded, totally: no attendant! A total lack of carefulness, ignorance of consequence, a trustful innocence. If he were at prayer, I wouldn't slay him, for that would catch him at Grace and send him dispatch to Heaven. Here now, like a heathen, he's bowled over laughing, ready for *dis*grace. Laughter is a sin, and he'll get *hell* for it once I deliver him from this life, which is now, while he's puffing in the gross, spasmodic rhythms of his hearty laugh. I'll cut him off, at this single stroke."

(Booboo rises, draws sword out of holster while King is laughing merrily on Queen's throne, bareheaded, having loaned his crown to Booboo. King laughs, amiably, at the "joke." While thus in his fit of stitches, and totally defenseless, unarmed but not in this instance disarming, he gets murdered by a stroke of Booboo's ferocious sword. This sets all havoc loose, as the royal rule is at an end. Now for the adventurers to survive, by their wits' supreme audacity.)

(New Act, same Scene, violence and turbulence on the stage, picture it, as chaotic mayhem replaces the King's authority. The King has died. Long live, then, the King. He's dead.)

(Booboo, still on throne:) "Well, it's over with, I've done it. I had glanced at my wristwatch hours before we planned to pull it off, and decided then and there that the occasion was a ripe moment, so my whistle I blew and faithful Clarence and all his retinue—my bold captain brave whom I'll promote to general today—came dashing in. Today is March First. I've stopped being pre-king. I'm the *real thing*, now!"

(Clarence, to Booboo:) "I'll congratulate you later, at greater leisure, my liege, on your royal investiture, to accession to throne by a high calling. We won't take this memorable moment lightly, I can assure. Meanwhile, whereas you've cut up Polski, *my* work is cut out for me and compels its business now to be done, urges rash action, such as cleaning out this palace of any leftover royal familyites and such that serve them." (Shouting to his troops:) "Attention, my men! Let's charge and attack. Let's kill at random. Let's be bloodshed-bound, on an unquiet riot. Booboo did what *he* had to, sooner than planned, but no less well done, as you can see by the carnage and the purple blood in a pool spreading from the slain King who wasn't on his guard and foolishly found us all trustworthy which posthumously he can only regret now for not sharing his wife's premonitions of suspicion. Let's go get *her*, men. And anyone else, too."

(Led by their leader, the rowdy battalion goes charging out, whooping it up, on an indiscriminate warpath, at liberty to do carnage in war's exceptional poetic license. In hue and cry, out they rush. On a wild rampage.)

(Booboo:) "Good, they're going out. Let them match *my* deed, multiply. I set a high standard, let them follow. All is set, and I'm here. I exult, I'm official. By grace of me, I'm God. Won't *Lady* Booboo be proud, to see me thus. Modestly I'll proclaim, 'Only did my duty, dear', shrugging to disclaim what I've done. She'll *insist* I did boldly, and well. I'll give in, admit she's right. Look at me here! Poland's God, its new king. It's me, believe it or not.

Well, I've taken action with my own hands, and answer only for myself. I'm not my mother's child any more. I've grown up, I'm mature. It's proven now. I've done what's rarely done. Who dare call it a crime, shall die! I determine what's moral, now. I'm the law, what I say goes . . . Always granted, of course, *Madam* Booboo's approval. She's my gross equal, her rank Majesty, the ranking female of the land once Clarence captures the *real* one and makes brief her widowhood by mowing her down. Her grief will be short, her mourning period so brief. She'll join him, at once, in royalty's dead dominion. She had inklings of this, never heeded. Her prophecy has been cut short: it's come too true: *so* true, her brutal end even now waits the vigor of Clarence, apprehending and dealing her the crowning resolution to conclude her awful prophecy.

"There they go, dashing out, and I'm at peace, I'll take a rest, on *my* throne. It's earned, I think. I took it to have deserved it, by guile, stealth, force, and valor. By right, it's mine. I'm here. This testimony is given on March First, and I'm the holy witness. As king I'm God. Nor mild my reign."

(There he sits dreaming, but fully awake. He's slightly tired, fat, and old. *Others* now take up the cry of vigor. Robust bodies, the uniformed rebels, led by plucky Clarence who wooed them from the regular army in a brilliant feat of recruiting to swell his reserves to amass confidence by such gain. He's trained them for their first hot moment now, on a blood quest. Their commission is a pleasure, ignoble glory. They're ordered unleashed, to the kill. They don't file out orderly, but at helter, abandoned, to disarray on an enjoyable fray. What a lark they romp on! They have the run of the place, to haphazard any chance of found prey, be it rank or servile, they have their way. They're not reined in. So they roll out, to rush about, soaking up irresponsibility, an army's mighty group-immunity to deeds otherwise evil that they easily may commit, their leader permits it, they're free of guilt. What a welcome charge! Discipline had been tedious. Now to make free, find what come. The louts are loose to overrun. They go about it merrily. *Polski's* merriment is stilled, it had been his last mood. Now the *army* takes it up. With lusty shout.)

(Here's the next Act, the Scene still essentially the throne room but also palace roaming by marauders all. All the rooms may be visualized, of the Monarch's residence, the hall of State, where Poland has situated her fate in ceremony and sovereignty. Today's a fatal day of change. A chaotic romp is about instead of sedate pomp. There's a radically altered circumstance, of frightful import. A coup on conspiracy hails in a new installed king who has usurped the fray and is ensconced, though not securely, for his rule sits unsteady, perilous yet till events are confirmed. His wife hasn't appeared yet. She bears decisive weight. Poised on precariosity, founded on fraud, plucked out of a game, taken from the King's laughter, the wrested crown, uneasy, having relied on ruse for its head-change, gleams and glitters. What awaits Booboo? Surely not retribution? Mere religious scruple, a Christian myth! He sits, others go wild.)

Clarence's men how pursue the Queen and the whole royal household, ministers and family and all retainers. They're on a slaughter hunt. The page gets sliced in their exit, and other court servants on their path. Anarchy is now loose. The center cannot hold. The throne room is empty of all life save Booboo who is seated on the King's throne, fully crowned. Beside him, the slain King is sprawled at the foot of the Queen's throne, emitting a puddle of blood. Fat Booboo sits, smiles. The conspiracy is working. He tastes success. It's delirious, it goes to his head. Thus begins his Monarch's-reign. He's head of state. Poland is in his hands. He holds the royal sceptre. The coup has been pulled off. He got away with it! His wife ought to be pleased. She's back in their residence, getting all dolled up. The day has started out glorious. This afternoon there'll be a military parade. As King, *Booboo* will preside. His first "official" appearance, in his new role. It suits him already. He can tell. He was *meant* to be King. It has the right *feel*, for him. He's a *natural*, at it. To *rule* is his true profession. But not the way Polski did. The new reign will be with an iron hand. A *tyrant* to be coronated. To culminate this afternoon's military festivities. The whole state will celebrate. Time enough, later, for general grief. Not for Polski, this grief: for the body populace; from pole to pole in this kingdom, grief will reign. Human life will be held at naught, belts will be pinched, austerity and suffering will be inaugurated. The Booboos shall institute prevailing woe. Poland has fallen, to its internal foe. When will Russia intervene? Not now. Meanwhile, *Clarence* must go. "Go" being a soft word, for "die."

First let Clarence complete his work, of bloodshed mighty. Then he'll meet his reward. And the handsome, promising young officer shall find his career nipped in the bud. Hope Mrs Booboo hasn't fallen for him; or she'd be furious! It's Booboo's reign. He came from far away. Now he's here, having made the most of being here. It's a fine triumph, so far: sweet-tasting. To *keep* it so, will be the argument of his new or-deal. To come into good fortune is fine. To maintain it—that's a *man*'s game. Is Booboo the man? More than that: *King*. Reality has surprised him: it's come true.

(Another Act, another Scene, the number lost count of. It's in the confused palace. Clarence's cutthroats are slaughtering at will. Clarence's central goal is the Queen, whom the royal psychiatrist has taken in tow. The psychiatric treatment ward is reached through a tricky corridor. Clarence locates it, and goes in, with his sword raised. He aims to add to the Holocaust, Polish nineteenth-century version. His unarmed foes are there as easy victims to that warrior of finesse whose promotion to general that night is guaranteed. Still in his captain state, he speaks:)

"Well, your Majesty, you're caught on the professional couch of your mental healer. Before I kill you, I'll give you the news. Sensational, not routine, news, and of special interest to you. King Polski was slain a few moments ago, as you had forecast, by my Lord Booboo. It ought to make you sad. From my point of view for self-interest, it's an agreeable turn of events that lauds me in my ambition. Declare your final statement, as you're about to be made 'late'. Am I in for a scolding? I toy with you, and dally. I wield mortal power over you, and find this amusing."

(Queen:) "This is highly sadistic of you. I had *known* Booboo for the bad man he is, but my dead husband saw only inflexible good in him. He wouldn't condescend to ignoble suspicion. As a result, I'm widowed. But only briefly so. For you'll send me out to join him, my deposed Polski, in our imperial heaven. I'm too stunned to weep. I shall look at death nobly."

(Still Queen, to psychiatrist:) "And so it turns out, you quack doctor, that after all I had no need of you. You were Freud-drugged as a fashionable dispenser of the latest depth therapy. Your services were beside the point, for I turned out right, and you owe me apologetic congratulations for my acute apprehension, undeluded, of reality before it happened. Is that 'sick' of me? Pessimistic, yes. But insane, no."

(Psychiatrist, abashed:) "Your Majesty was correct. My professional ethics prompt me to pronounce you 'sane'. I can give you a certificate to that effect, signed and notarized. But that would be too late. Clarence is intent upon your death, not to be deprived. I'm sorry you'll die. I liked my job while it lasted. It conferred a certain prestige, that did me proud. You were to be my first royal patient, in my glamorous rostrum of clients among the sick nobility of this—though esteemed—decadent court. Now Clarence swipes my occupation, by conferring on you a fate worse than mere neurosis or nervous anxiety: he means to put you to death. That would terminate your mind. As to your mental health, it's its final solution. I leave you to your emotional stability. I'll escape this room, like a leaking rat from a ship, as a surviving act, if possible. Spare me, Clarence; you block the doorway and bar egress. Why should your sword claim *me*? It's steeled for Her Highness, by sharp devotion. Let it bluntly let me go. I'm of slight consequence."

(Clarence, to psychiatrist:) "I dislike you, so you'll die on principle, or by the tinge of my caprice. How's *this*?" (Lunging a thrust.)

(The psychiatrist is mortally punctured by a straight jab of the captain's lusty sword, and dies in fright. That finishes *him* up, and Clarence now turns to the cringing Queen; emboldened by that small deed.) "Well, Queen, you're next. Are you scared?"

"Of course. Wouldn't anyone be? Mine is no enviable lot, at this instance. But I must submit. Already dead is my husband. I grieve, I mourn. Please let me change to black mourning weed. I want to die *properly* as a widow. I'll let you watch, while I take off my royal dress to bare my flimsy undergarments as I change into widow's garb. Wouldn't that thrill you?"

"I'm excited erotically by that prospect. It's so sinisterly stimulating! Let's go into your dressing chamber, get undressed. We'll have a brief bout of sex by mixing hot and wet: a timeless formula. What a capital idea!"

"I own it is, handsome Clarence. Please prove virile."

"Don't doubt me. I have ardor, *plus* experience, though in years young."

"I pant for it. But what *follows* on the agenda, after our orgasm? I dread what's to come then. I'll be nude and spent, at your disposal. What's your next ruthless plan?"

"Then I'll permit you to put on your black dress. Which I'll soon make red, by my sword's post-lust. It's so enticingly perverse, the whole act! My male tool is standing on end. Seduce me, please."

"I shall, Captain Clarence. In the modesty befitting my position, in a regal fall from dignity as my last pleasure before death. Would Polski have begrudged this to me and barred consent?"

"That's metaphysically debatable. I'm rearing to go. Come with me, carnally, darling."

(With his unsworded arm around her, Clarence escorts the Queen to her dressing chamber with its adjoining boudoir. He's thrilled, for she's royal. He's made a conquest that stirs his already vanity-laden head. It whirls him giddy. He loves his role among women: he's reached the top! Then to kill her, to rid him of her romantic clinging. How clean and convenient! How simplifying! It unclutters life, and leads to the ideal. Essentially, he's an idealist. But as a battling warrior, that's his means. He has style. He's attractive. He wins hearts. He kills, too. He's so versatile! He's a destiny-favorite. The obese Booboos are gross and vulgar: unfit, aesthetically, to rule. Opportunely, they'll be displaced in time, with *Clarence* as king! His ambition soars! Now, to a low act of lust, this sneaky seduction. His paramour is doomed. She confers royal favors on him; then submits to his sword blade in her widow's weeds. Decorum is observed. The King's memory has been respected, in a fashion, by some depraved veneration. What a First of March! Poland is steeped in snow, which fell yesterday. Snow being white, add some blood to it. It's also her black day. White, red, and black. That's the color scheme. Then add gold: that's the Booboos' dream.)

(Speaking of the Booboos, what of Lady Booboo? The next Act and Scene of this epic play is devoted to that fat English refugee. She's fated to meet her downfall. While Booboo had sliced Polski to take over the crown, Lady Booboo was getting dressed for the big day. She had expected the assassination to take place, according to schedule, later at the afternoon military maneuvers and state review, a formal and highly heralded occasion that was to be the fashionable event of the year for the social set. But Booboo had seized an earlier opportunity, with Clarence alongside and the hastened troops, to do in his pathetically trusting victim, whose want of suspicion might be deemed pathological, resorting to not the slightest security, seeing no need for it. Hence the early slaughter, on the spot, where the thrones were. Now Madam Booboo is heading there, in full and formal dress. She ascends the staircase, which the architect had spiraled long centuries ago in the Baroque flamboyance of taste. She's on her way up to join her conspirator-spouse whom she believes is in interview parlance with the King. Unknown to her, he's already attained his goal, through premature violence. She would be due for a surprise. On the way, though, she gets "waylaid." A rude soldier grabs her. It's a traumatic shock for her. As he grapples her to wrestle her down, she breathlessly but indignantly blurts out:)

"How dare you, you brute! Take your rotten paws off me. I'm his Lordship Booboo's wife. Who gave you permission to molest me? This is outlandish impudence. Is Captain Clarence your commander? If so, I'm *his* boss, and will have him punish you for this manhandling you've still not desisted from. You pest, request my pardon, or your rough behavior will be reprimanded in full, and you'll answer at the rate of your life for daring insubordination on these sacred steps of so sovereign a staircase that Poland's past ghostly kings and queens still frequent here when roaming up and down in search of nostalgia to bring their former rule back. I'm on my way to the throne room, at the top of this stairwell, for there my husband is in conference with His Highness, which is the measure of the respect *you* ought to accord *me*. You scoundrel cur! Now basely beg me for the mercy I might not give unless you beg from the well of humility and grovel in your humble place. Now serve me contritely with your tongue!"

(Soldier, in unrepentant insolence:) "Look, lady, only to Clarence do I owe submission. I'm obeying the orders he gave, so let me quote them at you. To us assembled troops in the crowded throne room scene he orated thus, with Marc Antony's own eloquence: 'Men', he said, 'King Polski is dead. Booboo slew him. I command you to run on unruly riot in all the floors and rooms, on an indiscriminate rampage, of this King's Palace. Slaughter anyone you see, on sight at random, who's not in the loyal cause of our uniform.' Madam, that includes you; which condones my conduct. The Captain continued: 'Don't watch out for who you're slaying, just slay. Abandon yourself to my solemn rule of anarchy. Go at it with a light heart, to purge this palace of the court we've overthrown, of all supporters and retainers whose allegiance was spent on the king now dead. I'm charged to tell you this, by great Booboo. He'll forgive you your extra violence: Charge it to his account.'"

"But soldier, I'm Booboo's *wife*! Can't you respect that!"

"You act exasperated, but I don't believe you." (Ogling her lasciviously:) "You're quite stoutly obese. It brings out the beast in me, or the best of me (good, better, bestial), for that's my prime taste, in the women, my fetish if you will. I prefer them gross, which is what *you* are. I've waylaid you, on my way. I will have gone out of my way to have laid you as well. Lift, lady, your dress: I want to see what's up there."

"Only *Booboo* has seen up there: how can *you* follow *him*?"

"Easy. I'll grab you by force. I'll indulge in a gentle rape. Are you prepared?"

(Melting, though in fear:) "What's your name? You're charming."

"I'm Private Anonymous: a blank version of my name."

"Rape me, but spare my life. You've filled me with terror."

"Now to fill you with my fleshy blade. There, I'm in. Can you feel it?"

"Oh, it feels nice."

"Good. Move around. Let's get into the rhythm."

"Oh, I'm passionate! What a lovely sensation!"

"Are you *glad* I took you by force?"

"Oh, you brute, you're so cruel!"

"Oh, I can't control myself! I'm about to come!"

"Can't you restrain a little longer?"

"No, the ecstasy has got me in its grip, in the rubbery flab of your coils, so soft to my firmness, so meltingly resistant to my bony hard length, it's unbearably exquisite, I can't hold out, I crave relief, ah—I come."

"There. Did you like it?"

"Yes. By the way, I'm a sadist pervert. Instead of grateful tenderness after our 'act', I feel belligerent, and will do you in."

"That's inhumane!"

"Well, that's me, all over. It's my very quality!"

"I implore you to spare me."

"That rouses me all the more, you ugly ship of blubber, to bruise you up and down." (He pummels her, with great brutality.)

(Collapsed:) "Oh, I think I'll expire!"

"Good. I had intended it. Now prudence is guiding me. I'll leave you lying here in a lump, as I gather myself up, spruce up my uniform, and bolt out in a dead getaway, leaving you here for dead. Good-by, you bulk. It was nice only for while it lasted. It was too quick, putting me in a rage, and I beat you up. Your condition is critical. You're slowly dying, barely breathing. You're a lump of lard. I enjoyed both laying and bludgeoning your body, which are its only twin uses for my limited palate of taste." (Sudden revelation, as an afterthought, on glancing at her inert form on the ornamental staircase so richly elaborate:) "Hey, you *do* look like Booboo's wife: you were right after all! I'll run away, so not to get accused. You're all broken up and bruised. You could never identify the culprit who did you in, me. By grace of that dullness, my undeserving life is saved for not being fingered by official investigation: you, as key witness, too close to death to testify. I'm spared to live and keep my guilt private. By recompense, the more devoted I am in my Captain Clarence's service, as a faithful soldier to new Booboo's cunning regime. I serve King Booboo! It's ironic, having just ravished *Queen* Booboo. Undetected, my crime goes free. Have a peaceful death, my lady. It was nice *laying* you. But *slaying* you was best. I'm good army material. I make an excellent soldier. For I'm not overly delicate. For war, that's good. War has its special good of virtues bad otherwise. I qualify, in the war-profession. I hope to lay and slay others, in the long course of my career. But never so high a lady, as thou. You've just become queen! Your royalty short-lived: due, I confess, to me. I'll never forget this. I'm a private in the Polish army. I'm alive now. I'm soiled, as an angel. Therefore spotless, as a brute. Today's the First of March. Our fields are strewn with white. A new head wears the crown, in our snow-laden land. I've deprived the crown of his consort. A villainous deed, whose cause I'll obscure, on this black day. Such infamy! I've contributed my share. I've done a heavy duty, in private, reducing the royal family by half. The more power is Booboo's: he has no mate to share it with. Will my leader Clarence wrench it away? He's just the lad to do it. It's likely to his character. What foul times we've fallen on! What's the *rest* of Europe like? Will there be a war abroad? I serve, to live and die. Long live his future majesty! *Clarence* I refer to; and I his follower. The crown is slippery. What trick is destiny up to? I'll live to see, but might die for it. A soldier can't take death seriously: it's too high, at a moment's notice. So I live sensually, while life's cheap form is still with me. I'll die craven or bold, in national duty. Not knowing it, I slew the brief queen: but unseen. It'll be my grave's secret. But let that wait. I breathe more violence yet, at age only twenty-three I'll die, one day: but mean to fill death up, by propitiation with others I slay, on the way, for *my* fatal day's drawn-out delay. I'll contribute others; then go myself. Spared, so long as I give. And when the giving gives out, then will my *living* be unstout. Down, then, will *I* go, a Polish corpse. With no historical monument to me: I'm consecrated to anonymity, unsung to the legendary glamor of heroism. The more *prominent* figures win glory: Booboo and Clarence, I refer to. I'm merely their knave: *how* knavish, may Booboo be preserved from, in my authorship of his wife's death. I bumped into her on the staircase, having confronted indirect. Then I turned brutal. She was my vessel, then my corpse almost. So I steal away. And slide out of sight. In dark privacy, I, a private, deprived my lady of her light and life, and I leave her, to live. Is there a message in this? Philosophy won't grow fat on it. Nor will fame carve its analysis for history. I did a dark deed, and flee. I embraced *her*; now, anonymity. My rape is over; my days not. I live; but meant another's end of stature vaster than me in courtly rank by a monarch's degree. Done is my prank. I ease away. Abstain from my punishment, God. I take anonymous refuge, lost among troops. I wear the uniform. It gives me a thousandfold concealment, for my battalion counts a thousand. I'm all thousand of them: one, and all. Army life is for me. It's not all dull. It can boast many a compensation. I just helped myself to one: the Madam Booboo that was. Adieu, gross Majesty. You'll stink like a fish. Meet your origin, of dim England, by the roaring Thames. It's sad for your life, that you're dead. But death gloats on it: soon, for you pulse yet, by the feeble beat. You were never beautiful, but great in girth. Now meet Polish earth: not the English sea.

"I steal out, and go. Cloaked by uniformity as an army man. *More* pillage is at hand. I hear the steps of troop-brothers. I'll join the ranks, in disarray. Clad in boisterous anonymity, that stalks the prey in the license of our fray whose day is still high with action as we riot and rampage to ravage where we may. *My* feast is done; I'll take *another* one."

(Soldier sneaks away. Lady Booboo is nearly dead. Clarence happens along, and gathers her up: *he* recognized her. Her weight is a pain in his arms. He bears her to the Throne Room, depositing her immense carcass at the foot of Booboo's throne; then, respectfully, stands aside.)

(Time for a new Act, arbitrarily put at Act One Hundred, unmathematically considered. The Scene is now taking place in the Throne Room; the characters being the former Polish King ((dead)), Booboo's wife ((not quite but almost dead)), Booboo himself ((crowned and throned)), and Clarence, young, with a promise in his future limitless and indefinite for what he can do, in his major road to higher being through the mess-enveloped business of low doing in lofty places for the power and spoils tenuous and for grabs. Clarence will be grabbing with a better grasp. Booboo has his delusion, now, a dream come too true, with retribution ahead. There's the near-dead carcass Clarence has faithfully delivered. The King's soon a bachelor. What freedom, to suddenly match the rule in unrivaled might! Clarence had killed off the remaining female Majesty, and now found the would-be female usurper closing in to the same condition of being unalive. This is a dear harvest of deaths royally received. So swiftly done, and more slowly believed. All happening to a foreign fat man on the Chair of Poland. How to accept and digest all this human news? His greed will hold him stout to all this. The grabbing looks good, with highly rated plucking, self-interest will restore order. Here's a still-living wife; she's done for without intention. What aligning plans can gain by this? Luck is providing much. Such givings, how taken?)

The unofficial king self-elect receives this jarring surprise: Booboo, alarmed, stupefied, but not without pleasure mingled upon discovering how his spoils are now undivided, and all his own, unshared with a dead wife who was a thorn and bully on his side, a domineering shrew. Now he's *rid* of her! That's as good as having killed King Polski! More power to him, fortune has provided well today. He's increased by a kingdom, and by the loss of a wife-pest. His property waxes great, with these growing additions to his already ample lot enhanced by these fortunate expansions. Uncontested king: only Clarence stands in the way yet, to absolute rule. Clarence remains, as a threat. To eliminate him, is the next step. Another vast boost, that would be, on the ill-gotten mound of prosperity. Booboo craves power the more he attains it. The ideals he never had are tarnished anew and wear recent blemishes of corruption absolute. He's fat and famous, and wants more. He'd like to be head of Russia, now! That means deposing a *new* king, a prime emperor in all the world. Booboo spoils to do this. It's to be his neighbor-policy as Poland's scheming king plotting further downfalls. He's a rebel-monarch, by contradiction. His throne is unsure. Only one security is left open: world domination. On Napoleon's or Caesar's scale, imperial, to colonize galore. He'd like his fame to spread; though ill-bred: all to adore his name, as Booboo the Great. And he'll kill his subjects who call him fat. He'll determine reality: he'll decree himself thin; and of Clarence-handsome dimensions; once rid of his helpful captain. In gratitude, he'll reward Clarence well: post him haste to hell.

His *wife* is going there, soon. Here she is, lying and dying. He gets off his throne, and tenderly kneels down beside her. Here's their final conversation. They're soon divorced by a great divider, she over into death, while he sucks living provider, to lay waste some more. Lady Booboo is pathetic, lying there. Booboo kneels down, and places his ear to hers. They'll whisperingly confide, with her dying strength, keeping death at fatiguing length. Will she reprimand him? If true to her nature, yes, but her nature is *going* so she may prove false. Their talk gathers length. Though alone—a hidden court stenographer records their dialogue: which, whittled down to basics, comes out sounding like this:

"I'm almost dead. So soon! Hardly queen, and having never enjoyed it. An ill stroke of fate, at such a mistimed annihilation. I'm leaving you, Booboo. First, let me recriminate you. You were my death's cause, you boor! By not sticking to our plan of *this afternoon's* assassination. An anonymous assaulter gobbled me up. While at it, he offended my decency, and undid my fidelity to you, though little did you deserve it. It feels bad to be dying. All the same, here it is. I'm going stoically. Fortitude is seeing me out. It proves my superior dignity to you, you fortunately living oaf! I hate you, husband. I'll haunt you after life. I'll harass you with guilt's plague, you'll see! I'll be an avenging harpy. You'll rue the day you ever met me. Yet I guided you to the throne. Without the incessant nagging I riddled you with, you would have become discouraged along the way and refrained meekly from the crime I made you do as the crown-assassin. Live in infamy in Poland's annals. I'll miss out on all the fun. What a pity! I *got* you where you are: for reward, I should have *shared* it with you. Now I'm left out. You hog, where's generosity gone? I taught you greed, or grew it bigger in you. We behold ambition attained. But in *woe*, I must go. Why not *you*, also? Well, *Clarence* will see to that. And very well, too."

"My queen, you're speaking silly. I'm moved to pity; but feel too full of terror to share your fate by volunteering to abdicate along with you. To the survivor, belongs the spoils. You're making me a widower. I'll inaugurate my administration by being coronated garbed in black. The whole kingdom will go in mourning for you. It will be by ordinance of me. I'll monumentalize your memory. When referring to myself, I'll say '*we*', in plural, '*our*', as the case may be. That's to include you, and do you honor. Can you appreciate it now? Or are you too preoccupied with your dying? Puff me out your gentle answer. Brief your reign, in grief my Queen. Now you're only a *has*-been. And you lose a husband. By embracing death's kingdom, a mortal act of infidelity. You cuckold me, with death! You lack chastity, your Grace. And an anonymous common soldier ravished you; after that betrayal he killed you. So I'm glad you're going. My revenge is complete."

"You wretch! I *hate* you! I met my death while on my way to join you. It was my greatest misfortune."

"Adieu, sweet Queen. The royal 'we' and 'our' in speech shall confer you language-immortality while I reign at court. It'll keep your honor alive, by indirect praise; you being on a par with me, in joint undivided Majesty. *Share* my kingdom, lady."

"I'm mocked, for no sooner am I Queen but imperial heaven is included in my sovereign range of divine overreaching. I attained premier rank; and leave *you* to enjoy it."

"Better me, than you . . . For *some time*, you've been about to die. You linger, and show no haste. I'm impatient. So out comes my sword" (He whips out his sword) "and in it goes in you" (Stabs her) "and out goes your life; and in I go, to worldly profit and material rulership. The *world*, now, is the limit. I covet no more. I'll attain it. Russia is next."

(With that audacity, the Act changes though the Scene remains. Clarence has been attending. He'll make his bid for a show-down with the new king whom he's just seen commit a second bloodshed in the same morning from the same ill-gained throne. Booboo lacks morals. He just does no matter what; for momentary self-increase. Booboo is a selfish new king. Clarence will defy him. Madam Booboo turns angelic from hideous, in the halo death places on evil's corpse. It's laid to Booboo's account a crime which Clarence is to hold against him, in their power-wrestle. The contest is on. One Booboo eliminated; and one sitting yet, caught red-handed by an ambitious young man who'll capitalize on the event to gain insurmountable advantage with so opportunely placed a pretext for righteous protest in an unrighteous cause. The power sways, where does the balance land?)

Clarence was witness, mouth agape. He stared at the hastening of an unmating. He would now reprove Booboo, for this offense to finicky sensibilities. He opened his Cupid-curled lips to dare criticize this act unfit for a king. But Booboo headed him off. Booboo felt foul and full, not to be fooled with, by a soldier's audacious tampering. His wife's mountainous corpse, like a beached whale, gluts the throne platform. Booboo nevertheless is seated on his throne, starchy and stiff with Egyptian dignity as depicted in extant hieroglyphics. Clarence is snarling. The regal room is otherwise unoccupied, but for two living male villains and a perished female one of recent issue. Plus a slightly older corpse of congealed blood, from which a good and trusting King escaped to a neutral and unPolish heaven. Ensues in vehemence this surviving debate:

"Look here, social climber. You've stolen a crown. I was instrumental, even paramount, in helping you. Now I claim to the full the rewards you promised me for my invaluable assistance. I want an instant pay-off. You're not scrupulous, nor by nature honorable; so I must forcibly remind you, and even extort what's due me now. *I* know the steep road you took, to your fine seat of eminence now. The way was as crooked as yourself. Your guilt is known by me, I can blackmail you. *You*'re armed with a sword, and so am I. Who's more deft, were we to duel mortally? Of course it's I. You can't dispute, I'm agile, in zest of mobility; whereas you're as stationary as a trunk whose circumference remembers the branches overhead and sinks sullenly into old roots. *I* have the edge. I *could* kill you, but I won't; if you resist, I will. That's *my* bargaining power. That's how we stand. With this background as an understanding, let's bargain and bicker, for these spoils of state."

"Clarence, this is a hard bargain you're driving. Let's be allies, not foes. Our guilt is mutual; so ought *we* to be, in common purpose."

"We're in this together? Surely. Your wife has left us. We two remain. Let's stick to each other. There's so much to gain, if we consolidate it. We must explain to the public—not just of Poland, but of Europe altogether—just why we deserve to have what we've stolen. We must put up a good front. The correct 'image' is vital, here. Outside the palace, the folks are clamoring. Rumor has reached them. They've received it with confusion. They want clear instructions how to interpret the bewildering 'takeover' we've pulled off today. My army and police are keeping them disciplined, checking them from mob massacres and riotous measures. We shall put out an official communiqué, a papal bull, or court bulletin, guiding their thinking on these unthinkable events. Booboo's sudden ascension to royal rule, Polski's also-sudden 'ouster', must tactfully get vindicated, if we value keeping our gains. I've instructed our public-relations staff what construction to put on this morning's seeming inexplicables. To this effect, Comrade Booboo: what we've done, however bloody, is by public approval, and on popular demand; we've acceded to the will of the people: we did it for them. Here in this nineteenth century, what we've succeeded in our drastic coup to inculcate as reforms ('much-needed reforms') are these I list: the liberation of serfs from time-honored bondage; the freeing of peasants from degrading toil in abject servitude; workers rescued from subjection to hasty bosses; the reform of a crippling bureaucratic paralysis that's kept Poland behind the progress of the Industrial Revolution that, beginning with England, has swept the more enterprising nations to uniformly enriching effect; emancipating the middle-class of our backwards land from the noble condescension of their exploiters; unbinding the lower nobility from upper aristocratic dissolute predatory persecution; and finally, our releasing, our benign deliverance, of the whole aristocratic class from Polski's cynical 'patronage', which was exploitation pure and simple to bloat the royal coffers at the expense of those lesser in rank. Ours is a new humanitarian, reformist, liberal, 'will-of-the-people' regime of democratic principle for the good of all. The welfare of each Pole is the sole concern of the new sovereign, who's a *Saintly* King, called from henceforth 'Royal Saint Booboo', loaned by God above to improve the intolerably impoverished, ruinously retrograde, ignorantly unenlightened and blighted conditions of the Polish hibernating state. Poland shall awake! Thrive! Be enterprising! Become great! That's what my crew of public relations experts shall preach with the effective latest advertising techniques, launching a lofty propaganda campaign to vindicate our good name and silence our opponents and gag skepticism as to our most benevolent intentions in usurping the kingdom from the foolish dead Polski. Our regime has its apologists, already. They're hard at work, impressing on the public mind a climate of opinion favorable to our hard-won efforts. You'll be instated, and cleared of doubt. What an auspicious inauguration! Now it's noon. Let's feast on some lunch.

"Madam Booboo, Polski, and Polski's wife will be omitted from joining us due to their having incurred the discommoding inconvenience of what in polite circles is known as death. I myself, in fact, made love to the recent Queen—not yours but Polski's— before ending her time on earth. The sequence is what fascinated me. The act of love, followed straight by what ends all acts: her murder by my hand. I confess this, Saintly Royal Booboo, because I'm careless of what you think. In *titular* style, you're Poland's ruler, nominal. But I'm yours, actual. This is the priority I insist on. I control the army and police force. You're in *my* hands. I *suffer* you to rule; I have the power over you of swift death should you by chance disobey my any edict. *Follow* me, but don't lead. I take precedence. That must be clear. This is by straight command. Agree now, to agree always. Go ahead, fool. Swallow your pride. I grant you a *show* of vainglory. *Real* power resides *here*" (pumping own breast), "and now weakly show me your consent before I permit us further procedure."

"You win. Yes."

"Fine. I'll be loosely strict with you, as your lenient superior."

"I'll play your game, Clarence. We'll lunch now, preparatory to my official inauguration this afternoon, the coronation festivities and the military review, the show of our might and power, of our national unity, of strength at the helm of government. The parade maneuvers, attended by our Russian guest the Czar and his highest brass of staff that closely cluster round him, shall be truly a spectacle. The sun is out to melt the snow. We're greatly in; and out the old shall go. What I crave is gold. Shall I have it, dear Clarence?"

"Loads of it. I'll bestow on you the gift least of all counterfeit: Poland's treasury stored up in the sealed stacks and underground vaults of our most consecrated *mint*. Will that solace your greed, seeing how all *power* is mine, so that I leave avarice to your stead? You're a maniac swine in your miser's rutting heat for gold, which is a concentrate of money. Your late wife showed no slack of eager zeal for it herself. Instead, she's wound up empty. I see her bleeding. She's our moral lesson."

"It offends my sight."

"But *you* committed her soul to that sad state. It's *your* responsibility that her body is now declared a void."

"There you're inaccurate, Clarence. You found her yourself closely breathing her last, slumped down on our elaborately fantasy-wrought ornamental staircase, and you lifted her heavy hugeness and brought her to me, where she and I had our slight concluding argument to terminate our lifelong marriage argument, when I gave her a dispatching nudge with my trusty sword finalé to help her off this mortal coil in her slipping slide, her gasp of agony and distress. Without me, she would have been gone only five minutes later. I mildly hastened the event, with the slightest of shoves to one already dying. I'm then innocent. And in my innocence, a *wrath* shall burn!"

"For what or whom does your crowned obesity conceive such strange wrath? You're glad rid of her; yet you affix blame?"

"Though pleased she's no more, still my esteemed wrath must condescend anger on the common foot-soldier whose impudence and sodden lust made me a cuckold half an hour before a widower and castigated my honor with the rape he inflicted upon my consenting wife which made it no rape but adultery and a forced loss of faith. My dishonor *weeps* for revenge. The hour my wife died, she betrayed me! This I can't forgive. This is a king speaking! Which gives outrage articulation!"

"You're screaming, King. Tone down. What do you propose?"

"I'm righteously out of temper, frenzied. A slur and smirch upon my honor! This disgrace is an infamy! A warrant I shall put out, in my fuming indignation, for the apprehension, arrest, and torture of the common foot-soldier, that anonymous Private so-and-so, who did that villainy. I shall post a huge reward; he shall be turned in by a tempted informer. My spies will put a ring of investigation around the whole military corps, and with the reward on his head I won't rest long but will be short restless till the bastard's arrest. Sweet will his punishment be, to atone my *own* guilt. He's my scapegoat, in this. Then my wife's ghost won't come haunting me the way her real person all my life nipped me with a shrew's tongue. My conscience will be at peace, when that soldier becomes my victim. In so being, he'll be *her* victim, absolving *me* from her vindictive curse. Let him be in my stead when her wrath comes visiting to settle old scores with spiteful reckoning. That soldier is my salve; letting me escape from the harpy my wife shall be in the nether region. Her death lives in me. Let it not sign up me for an *also* death. I beg to live, and by atonement the soldier shall be sent as fit sacrifice to her altar. I recruit him as my altar-ego, my derogate (or surrogate or delegate) culprit for my wife's spirit to feed on as I safely fly away. For I fear her, in her death, to echo the fright her *life* gave me. From that nemesis, may my flight succeed. Clarence, does this seem irrational in me? Is it irrationality that I betray?"

"Completely. You're the perfect model of it. Compared to you, I'm suave as a snake. While you're a bull or buffalo or clumsy ox that buffets about and clouts himself. You'd make a fine court jester, King! You're a clown, but a wicked one."

"A *crowned* clown, if I'm one. It's my illegally confiscated prize. Here I'm sitting here. This throne is mine, which seats me below; and mine this crown, that the gods bestow. My predecessor (peace rest his bones, with his body spent there slumped down by the Queen's Chair) indulged me a privilege of *playing* at king (The *play's* the king: my conscience a thing.), with these two toys of golden semblance: crown and throne. Suddenly my sword turned what's playful to what's real! It's a game no longer, but earnestly I'm identified by it, which *you* even recognize. It's *true*, Clarence."

"Exult and crow, your Majesty. Still will your trembling show. You sit tentative. I *bid* you rule. Though younger, I'm your lord. The reins I control. You have *titular* might; what's *actual*, is mine. And so our unequal share goes. Between us, I fear for Poland. A passing brave show it would put on. I plan the conquest of Russia. It seems difficult: yet my fate shines magic for a star. I have some amazing hope for it. Bold deeds in our hazard have we capped off. My confidence surges for more. I'd take Russia, if I could. The Czar will be our guest on our parade grounds right by here, by the palace estate. His chief ministers will attend. I intend to kidnap them, for ransom of all of Russia. This *seems* ambitious, and it *is*. It's to test how great I am. I *claim* greatness, and wait to realize it with a supreme dare against that furry monster, the Russian bear. The scheme of this audacity, plainly, exceeds any crime that the twin Booboos ever plotted on the woven climax of their dream. Greatness is *mine*. You're a silly comparison, Booboo. I heavily laugh at you. *My* gain comprises Europe, in scope; yours has ended on this mock throne. Know your place, knave. *My* place is nowhere, since infinity spins it. I'm a handsome youth whom girls adore, and the recent Queen who's no more, the rightful one, whom you widowed and whom I killed off in mourning weed after clutching her in the tight breath of nudity. My destiny is more than royal: the world's a garden where I'll pitch my empire, snug and globular like her

Majesty's girdle I took off prior to my rapt possession of her. Possession I desire, of the female *Earth*: she can't resist me—*no* woman does. This is *credible*, not raving. Heed me well, my monarch: the name of Clarence will eclipse that of Caesar, and shade Napoleon off. History has met its measure: I've come to conquer Time. All preceding fames shall die, in the new rise of mine. The universe had a chronicle, till now: I conclude it. All ends, when *I* end. And my end is not."

"I'm awed. But you have symptoms of megalomania, as well as *hubris*, which is unbecoming pride and a lapse of humility offensive to the gods. For all you aspire, isn't *failure* possible?"

"Failure doesn't exist. It's not known to me. My prior success goes gathering a dynasty. I'm only a young man. But what an old world it will be, when I'm through!"

"I dare not doubt you. Fear crushes me, when you *soar* so."

"I fly! I'll tear down the sun!"

"Then what *warmth* will we have?"

"Warmth by *me*! The sun being my province, *I* shed, *I* illumine. *I* let the stars dance, and present a full moon. *I* culminate astronomy. *You* can have Poland; Madam Booboo has death; and *I* have everything else!"

"Vainglory is a sin. You go too far."

"My star blots out all sin . . . But my stomach needs meat. I glide down now; perch on *earth*, a short while: long enough to eat. Then this afternoon's big ceremony, the Czar attending, and you coronated. Behind the scenes I'll do my busy work. I'll announce Russia mine, soon. That's more manpower, to take over India, Scandinavia, France, and Germany. Then we'll enter the New World, for our minion; and go below down Africa way. As a conqueror, I'm vastly avant-garde. I need more scope. Desire points the way. Attainment clarifies it. And clarity is my radiance. And radiance leads to God. And *God* I'll take away! He's only another name for *me*!

"Yes, Booboo, *have* Poland. And to your wife, Death belongs. But to me, all the *rest* goes: such dominions, that *territories* are no measure of, nor do *zones* declare, nor yet *hemispheres*, or tiny *con-*

tinents. All I want is Space. And Space includes Time. There, my ambition rests. Below that, I leave the rest. My grandeur knows no tower fit for *one* horizon, but captures what God did, to its absolute scheme on a matchless design. You took away from Polski what was his. Well, God's my Polski: his rule's mine, soon; all His Providence is my neat bag, my confidence trick, snatched like an apple. It's no act of burglary, but a cosmic revolution that converts ideals to their realities under my proprietorship and absolute hold. I'm a real estate wizard with an undividing province to take up till Totality at last reduces itself to declare its holdings and turn itself over into my dominion. Then my work is done. I'll take a rest, being All. And All will rest. And Clarence is the All. And at perfect rest, we stop. *Then*, what will heaven do? It's out. In me went *that* power, of full investment. What I was, and what I did, involved whatever had existence. In *me* went control. And my going means *all went*. But that's to be, though in the future tense. Till then, I've got a lot to do. Let's begin, shortly. First a little lunch, and then the Czar. And then to a *larger* star. We're not waning yet, when we *do*, *all* wanes. What will be brought down, heavily, when *I* go, is whatever else is. That sounds complete? In very broad terms? Well, I *operate* big. Why should I trifle?—the solemn comes first. I'll take it and end it. It's all-reducing of whatever's less, for the Void to fill. And the Void's my goal. When I land there, all is still. For God shall have done His will. And my nothing is the last to conclude, when ruin is complete. And the face shall be empty, of what world we know. Having begun in *Poland's* land. And put to doom, by *my* hand."

"Your speech expands abstractly and tears down limits where metaphysics stops short. It's infinite, but destructive, so far as your report clears its fathoming. Your youth holds such genius! Why was your career an army one? A professor you could be, in all that's occult. You could find a mental alchemy, given common ingredients and using only given elements. Or you could batter down philosophy, by pouring excess past logic into a world which reason may discover as the Spirit's dwelling place in its revealed vacancy. Or what a theologist might you have made!, a divine seeing holiness in the unlikely places. Or an astronomer you might have been, lifting up the sky to see it closer on its pouring down of details that barely get past the first eye. As a scientist, explorer, archaeologist, or one versed in mathematics, you would have extended progress to the state of grace that ignorance holds. And as a poet, who knows?—Your words might have imposed unsuspected orders on obvious and ignored things. That's a fantastic realm you have, in your reaching mind of thought. You could have cured disease and purged bodies of their carnivals of pain; even altered anatomy, to give man a better shape for the functions that must circulate. Defiant of these potentials, you chose militarily, and now aggress into statesmanship. Along the way you've collected maidenheads or renewed them in lapsed virgins by reversing experienced women into girls blushing their first ecstasy. Never had I considered you so extraordinary; never had you proven so. You expand articulation past borders known by method, till you force new content into old forms and put a face of fiction on foremost knowledge. Your impatience growls outside Poland's boundary, bored with what already is, wishing settlement in regions not attempted, to civilize zones of emptiness by the colony you breed mentally. What you touch goes cultivated, converted from the barren. I can't calculate what you do, or by how; but I give way when miracles turn eloquent. You're Merlin or Prospero, with a wand of tricks. Reality must jump at your bidding. No Russia could repress you, for your energy defies all. Truth gives way when your barrage pokes it; transformations make myths from anything you wish, and the legendary is copulated into its never-before. You're one called Clarence; you're all, beyond himself. My awe now is leapless. I'm your spectator for my life's remainder, for studying you achieve marvels by what's beheld. The Czar is no match for you. He's bound in time and caught by space. You stay free, and vary stitches along the net of all Being. You spy the pattern for detecting God, whose roam is invisible otherwise. Never such as you have I known; I thought you were a villain my size, bound only to material gain. I see you exceed me; so I take back place. My wife is gone, you're here instead. This change is welcome. I never swore to be content, as lesser than another. I'll go along as your Sancho Panza, or in any form you wish. Commanding is natural in you, for you're its *gift*.

"And Poland was the site of you!, of all birth places. Poland never did so well. Earth never knew your like. You've turned out, to mutate such a rarity the species holds no precedence for in all the contours of evolution whose detours devolved from a central origin to proliferate where no end is known. Man was only himself, till *you* came hence, the teacher and the lesson. You've cured me of my lust for gold. Beholding you is *mental* gold, and digs a miser's well in the fertile Spirit's ground. Do what you will. There's nothing to oppose this energy you bring into things. I'll be your vassal, though nominal king. And you, what conditions will clad you, to slightly veil or filter your boundless infinities behind? Nature made Clarence. But Clarence lifts nature. Toward what stop do we head? I'm being surpassed by every thought which you plant of seeds of your casual breath. My education is you, by what your path blazes to reveal, by tracings of labor that idly you spend. Clarence, I'm converted. Where are you now?"

"Everywhere by the here defined. We must lunch now with action prepared. The gathering already conglomerates for the drill of passing arms and a military show of might. A crowd swells the scene, as our window will show, This afternoon means taking Russia: no ordinary event of Polish feat. I'll stride it, by will alone, and deed's exercising of it. My greatness drably needs its proof to find a being born from only potential. Matter shall materialize in our manifest. There our ideals shall go clad, and goals find solid embodiment. Let's see what I can do. I'll eat for strength; then I'll end the day in historical creating. We'll put out the Twentieth Century as waste product grown incidental to current intention. I'm a figure for history. In me its works find a personal form. Events are in my molding. Their significance is mine. All this enfolding is now, once I get going. Fate is in my clothes: I carry it past the sentry, being its wooden horse. Through me the centuries shall rise in their defined pasts and those not wrought yet. I convey. I must be a sturdy vehicle, for so much to pass by in my gathered cloth. I'm the future, already. So it's time."

(The climax approaches. Clarence and Booboo eat, in readiness to change the world. The next Scene is big pageantry, grandeur's stirring act. The military festivities are underway. Booboo is proclaimed King. But he's dressed all in black! The announcer says it's mourning for the new King's barely-dead wife. Monster ceremonies are being conducted. A drill of armed might is maneuvered by the new General-of-State, whose post is also now Prime Minister: Clarence, whose uniform is the envy of all, in a daring mixture of colors. Hearts flutter, owned by the whole female sex. The Scene is set. The Czar attends, and Kaiser too, Prussia's head. What comes next? It's building, to . . .)

"Attention, all present." (The soldiers stop marching: the guests and citizens, those honored and those curious, listen. It's the new King speaking. He stands up like a bulging ball. Thousands heed. He proceeds:)

"Allow me, subjects and foreign dignitaries who honor us by visiting us, to give you a self-introduction, of who I am, not to mention other explanations I owe you, in bewildering matters that stand before us. I'm addressing a huge gathering, yet am not a public Speaker. Still, I'll try.

"I'm the successor to your old King Polski whose tyrannical reign mercifully ceased this morning. I did you a favor, by killing him. Your gratitude is a lifelong debt. As it's owing to me, I'll take it out in taxes. Then you'll *really* be in debt.

"My style is candid. You deserve my honesty, so I'm dealing it out. Do I shock you? Feel glad I'm your new King. Here's why. The old one was no good. His administration was your yoke. You were being pushed around. Now let *me* do it.

"I'm giving a speech to herald in a new progressive Poland. You'll have to pay for it by increased suffering. It'll be worth it: for *me*, not for you. My gain is your loss collectively. I like it that way, it justifies my power. I *love* power. But wait. It's *nominal* power I have. I'm *ceremonially* your king. The *real* one is in the wings. He's this charming man, who's standing by my side looking slightly surprised as well he might. To him is my allegiance in duty sworn. He's great Clarence, you know: captain till now, and behind-the-scenes agitator who schemed this coup and pulled it off by dint of a clever and active mind. He's my Prime Minister, and he rules me. He's your leader through me. In *him* is power. I wear by title my crown. He's absolute, and stands outside title. He's so good-looking. His prowess with the ladies has led to a scandalous reputation, giving him a notorious flavor. He's Poland's Lover. My admiration goes to him. His rule applies to us all. We must heed, or he'll kill us."

(Clarence descends to lower platform where he takes the seat of honor, looking up to listen seriously while the black-clad King-in-mourning fatly goes on praising his young accomplice in rousing tones and orotund grandiloquence:)

"He's General in command of our army, to take effect immediately. And he's the brains of our State. How can I praise him? My words fall far short. My slavish devotion will shower obedience on him. His will is my conqueror. I advise *you* to submit, as well. This includes everyone listening, not just our patriotic countrymen the Poles, but everyone else here present: from the Czar down; no exceptions allowed. Give Clarence the world, by making him the gift, voluntarily first, of yourselves. He'll take everything else. His destiny quite roars, to a special unlimited sphere. Make way, accord him what's his; if you shirk in this, it's to your peril, I warn. Clarence can be quite brutal, at times, in his ruthless power quest whose goal stops nothing short at world dominion altogether. This is the medal his fate wears on his proud breast, donated by history. We must follow with our faith. Let him lead us by the nose.

"No, no, stop that uproar. Are my words antagonistic? Well, you're trapped by my troops if you take it into your heads by force of mass to overrule my Lord Clarence in his ascendancy over us all; we must give in, for his star is dominant beyond our power to oppose. Let's all be led by him. You Czar, and you Kaiser, and you the King of England, and you the Austrian Emperor, and all you other pretenders, are in one man's hands, as I too am, it's Clarence controling us. Of us he makes his beginning, toward the world. Once he has *this* world, he'll pursue others, with the help of all the women, the fluttering petticoats of his admiring idolators who adore him till death—theirs not his. Clarence has captured permanent life: he's young enough.

"I have been describing a paragon that's indescribable, and on his behalf I will pass on what our youthful Master has in store, of concern to us all. He bade me to say that the world's capital is henceforth Poland. We'll permit each of the rest of you to continue speaking your national heritage language, whether its tradition be English, Russian, German, Spanish, or so forth. Poland has become central. This is primary change number one, over the established universe. It wouldn't be nice to refuse Clarence this: it would hurt us, and he wouldn't let us. Whatever his brain dictates is for us to carry out. This is the second principle I must state. It's as sacred as a commandment. World dictator, Clarence is. By all that are we so much reduced. We have a handsome leader. He'll make your lives ugly. But that's of no account, since your lives have anyway a short span. You're all bound to die. Only Clarence is exempt."

(Clarence rises to take the rostrum to stand alongside his rotund eulogizer. Beautifully dressed and slim of waist with gorgeous legs in tight military array, the proclaimed Emperor contrasts startlingly with the puffy beast of a new king. Hushed, the audience awaits their Master's voice. It will ring and reign, to knell their doom.)

"Thanks, trusty clown. I thought you were betraying me. I heard you say that I'll make the lives of our listeners and their brethren 'ugly', a phrase which I abhor. You ill represented me, Booboo, and for punishment I commit you to my improvised verdict, sentencing you extremely to death as the cost of your life itself. That leaves *me* in charge, only, as it does away with such clumsy assistance your nouveau royalty of parvenu kingship has unseemly submitted. I can do without it, you're only a cumbrance, a low and insolent nuisance murderously playing at king.

"In view—in *full* view—of our collected audience here in this epoch-smashing event that makes the historical hysterical in the world's lengthy dalliance with time (a flirtation consummated into a disillusionary affair), I'll have you beheaded. You tried to be my spokesman, but end up as simply any victim. Your rise to become king has this for a stop. Lady Booboo your wife died also today. Go you join her. Likewise King Polski whom you deposed, and his prophetic Queen, were also today slain. March the First is proving bloody. Will the bath continue?"

"A reprieve, Clarence, your pardon I request. Spare me from a a disgrace so public. Should I be beheaded in front of such an audience, I'd, frankly, lose face."

"You lose your face when your head is lost, as the removal of your soul will attest. What a swelling belly you have! The more a feast, then, for death. Death shall dine coarsely, I'm afraid, on so gross a stomach as you possess. Today is death's gluttony. *You* may be had, as its sumptuous dessert. Let *your* example end the feast, we hope. The audience will take care in their scare not to follow suit. The melting snow is in our sun. Today Poland glows. And I'm its cosmic link. My greatness shall not be local, but global. *Other* nations must co-operate. *Russia* shall fall first, it's so handy. It's right across our eastern border, so we claim it. If they resist, the Czar will die, who's in our hands today on a state visit, with his top ministers also trapped here, as distinguished captives. The German Kaiser and English King and his Holiness the Pope and the Austrian Emperor are ours too, for our troops are muscular. I enjoy this 'taking over'. It brings out the 'power complex' in me. I'll take on a hundred mistresses; no wife yet—why complicate my life?: I'm just starting out: an enterprising bachelor, slightly given to ambition. I intend to *win*: to boast idly, is for *Booboo's* stature. Mine succeeds, his fails. I please, he repulses. I'm favored, he's not. Fate *is* myself: so I needn't seek it.

"I'm making my public confession—with the armed might of forces to implement my every word, I'm born today. It's *others'* death-day, to celebrate my coronation as a human sun.

"I see here that Booboo is straining to make me debate him in so public an event. He's dying to interrupt me. *He*'ll be interrupted by his dying. I'll rid myself of his dubious alliance, that seeker after gold who'll end up with maggots. Frankly, Booboo, you're despised by me. That's the only reason I need to put you to a justifiable

54

end. What's your last testimony, and your trivial defense? Speak, putrefaction!"

"You're ungrateful and too proud, and your downfall will be your doing away with me, if you do. I ask you not to. Don't turn against me. We came a long way—you, me, and that repulsive lump of flesh for whom I'm such a conspicuous widower today as the sun glares off us on a nineteenth-century afternoon featuring March First from a snowy yesterday high in Poland's might. Kill me not, Clarence: the *gods* will protest, and avenge me. I warn you imperatively. There's *so much* of me, in the round, of great bulk and flesh. It's all meant to be *preserved*, please. My defense rests. May your mercy rise."

"My thumb is down, on your appeal. I condescend only to *reject* you, and wave your plea aside. Hideousness, prepare to die. It won't be fun . . . Yes, it will—from *my* viewpoint. I'd be delighted to have you off this earth. It would leave more room for *me*."

(The Scene is now the same, about two seconds later. The Act has advanced, however. This is the fault of the play *not of the sequence of events. A play has to be broken up, scene replacing scene, even a self-scene's own replacement. Plays are artificial. The events they depict are, all too decisively, real. It's a real afternoon there, a shining sun to lend it reality. Clarence is the speaker before a docile audience both imported abroad ((therefore foreign)) and domestically Polish of the realm native. High drama is taking place. Clarence is an attractive figure; even ((metallically considered)) "magnetic." Women sigh after him; others die, before him. One such is now to be, in his fall from fortune's rise, Booboo the Obese. But he's a king!, you say? So what?, there's no difference. Clarence wants it that way. Clarence gets what he wants. He's tops, here. His prime is all powerful: he has the power to put to death a king! And to kidnap Czars and Emperors for ransoms of national conquest! These are for no low stakes. These are for elevated chips. He's fascinating, Clarence. He's undergoing an expansion. Hear him, in the magnificent virility of his omnipotent gesturing based more on being than on the aping gesture. He is. What more can be said?)*

"History is myself. It's recorded *as* me. I want my soldiers (this is an *order*, though in public) immediately to disarm the bodyguards of all Kings, Emperors, Czars, and Popes here present, and all their Ministers as well. That will elevate our security, so that fear will have retreated from the proximity of our person. I'll be free to be. My being will serve destiny, enacted by me, to affect all people whose residence is currently in the world, fanning outward from this holy site of my enshrining.

"Do I violate international codes of ethics in taking prisoner the world leaders who had come as my guests? My disobedience to old laws is merely obedience to my own new laws, for as I go along I see fit to make and break. I'm made that way; let the *world* give way. My making paves the way for others' breaking: they must pay! I bear an expensive will.

"Now the heads of state from abroad have been bound by my swift-working men; is my hospitality at fault? *I* hadn't invited them. Two regimes ago Polski bade them come. One regime ago Booboo gave them welcome. *I* now preside; and take them as enemies. Swift doings have been going on in Poland. Events are taking a whirling tide. I must hustle to keep pace, or be left in the lurch.

"Fickle fate is mine today.
I'll *marry* it, to bid it stay.

"I always like to avoid the temporary. The permanent is more reassuring, when I can secure its enduring favors in such solid that I can break the will of time that tends to shove favorites aside.

"I legalize my crime, were any committed today. I have authority of being always right. Here high on this stage, I've had Booboo bound. The beheader is here for him, with rather a dashing blade. It will amuse my audience, or else chill them, to hear this concluding dialogue between the beast doomed, and me gallantly fortuned to this crest of all positions in the wresting of power away from rivals of eminence. First let's pause for a snack. Refreshments are to be served. The banquet, please!"

(A popular rumble of approval is heard. Clarence has scored again, in his right instinct to win people over. Waiters and servants move trestles of food in upon each row, generous portions for people to help themselves. There's a general adjournment for this repast, and anyone interested is shown discreetly to near-by bathrooms which the occasion has fabricated. Clarence has people's moods feeding of this will, and his gestures are going down well.

The bound heads of state are spoon-fed by their captors, so even *they* don't go hungry. Poland is host to friend and foe. Clarence is well in; all else falls out. Is his a *kept* advantage?, not flimsy like Booboo's? It's a mild afternoon for March First. The female weather, though lacking human form, is enamoured of this male Prince. He rules by charm; nature woos his ends herself, and makes them hers. Nature and Earth are both feminine; so how can Clarence lose?)

(The Scene remains; a later Act comes on, as the play's progressive motion seems somewhere to go, but "where" has its end unseen, as Clarence takes over from the taking over by Booboo of Polski's former reign which was only this morning just ended in a dazzling sequence. The chronology blazes by. Can Clarence endure? The tableau is all his, now. Is he capable of a fatal slip, like the crowns he's succeeded? Or is he a destined *Prince, as a dynasty's forebear provided he's personally susceptible to mortality? Let's follow, for well he leads, his brash swagger graced by elegance and dignity. Will the world yield to his sweeping insolence? In what rank does his greatness pitch its magnitude? His star brightens. Is it a vanishing flare? Or will it so illumine, that night days itself before our eyes and the Prince beams a sun's rays to make believers of skeptics? Booboo has fallen. Clarence takes over. His own modesty is far from humble. The audience has concluded its meal, and now dines off Clarence in his leaping tongue. Nimbly, what tricks shall he shower at them? All are bewitched, in thrall to this enchanting royal birth self-proclaimed. How high will his height go? Is his flight spared from its leveling out on low reversal and the fall that befalls all? The Prince and his miracle versus the unromantic world's bland average with time that conspires toward the commonplace. This mythic Clarence against dullness-inclined reality allied to time that evens out whatever's up and hauls down what soars for the flat fate of the mediocre to which the great must succumb from their privileged seat suspended among the immunities. But should Clarence fall to earth, the earth will fall for him, being female and unable to resist this lad who lightly dances upon consenting breasts. Back to the palace grounds, and the immensity of a spectacle, an amazing assembly addressed by youthful royalty self-wrung from the officer ranks. New power fascinates. Will its hold not slip? Will March First remain forever, to keen history arrested on the spot? The epic closes in. Eternity is focused on the new paragon. Will it halt variety and say "Stay"? Or will it neutrally allow all this to pass by? Will fading even find Clarence to happen to, now proudly clad in Princely form? On with the play. Gross Booboo is bound, death-bound to join his wife when Clarence sig-*

nals to the beheader. Will that coarse life have to go? To rid the stage of all that? For Clarence to remain, and both Booboos dead, and both Polskis, that had been far ahead?, now surpassed by a blinding flight to fame with Clarence its name, more than man, excelling proportion's risk by stretching luck to audacity's breaking point? Has he come too far, too fast, taking on more than he can bite off, speed too reckless for prudence to flag down with warning? Is he riding for a fall, and his might about to crash? We'll giddily track him, on his maddening course. He turns to Booboo with no mercy. He utters power in each word. "Death" is pronounced with Booboo for an object. The latter won't take it lying down, but oaths a curse:)

"I'm Booboo bound. Behold me in my disgrace. Clarence has sentenced my doom, and up here on this stage with me is an executioner with his portable blade that's meant to sever me from my neck, ingratitude's slice, a cut of unkindness that gives Clarence his callous calibre to call his character out as that of a bad opportunist gifted with good looks but his luck can't last.

"I despair, I grieve, that reluctantly this is my farewell speech. I take leave from Poland and the world. At least I'm going out as a king. It can only briefly console. I have a long eternity ahead.

"As I go, I'd like to hurl a curse. Clarence has granted me the freedom of these last words.

"He graciously will stand aside, permitting my final diatribe. It's venomous, loaded, upon him. My after-death shall plague him. My stout ghost will inherit my swollen and furious revenge, to inflict on the crowned head of this self-ordained Prince who's outliving me at his risk; though he grins his cynicism and humors me my outburst as the ravings in sorrow of one demented to have to go. I *do* regret to leave Poland. It was to be the seat of my empire. I was throne off. I was intermediary, between Polski and Clarence, all on one short day. That's the sole line history will accord me. Let me divulge more, for posterity to mold its notes on, when assessing my reign so short. I'll confess, and bare my booming bosom of its sweet will and long testament.

"I was a pre-king. Now all that remains is pre-death. In between, I'll say what befell. The crown relayed from Polski's trust, through me, to the one deemed Prince now. I accuse him of arrogance. Where is he heading? On a collision course with his own disaster. My oration will conjure this spell upon him, with a pre-funeral oath. Once I'm gone, he'll have terror for a bride. He'll find it hard to curb her.

"I orate pre-funereally on my soon demise. I'll spend a self-tear, down my cruising cheek.

"I mourn me to go, and am black-garbed to mourn my own wife: not knowing I was dressed for two. Due to Clarence I'm this economical. I owe him a small irony.

"Pardon, I bow my head, to let sentiment wash me over. This is no shameful display; is not a fat man entitled to sensibility?

"Much obliged for your indulgence. I had to give way. I sob that my life is lost. I took the crown away. How bereft my own head must seem. Ambition crowned me, but greed went to my head, in stolen authority. Now my *head* is to go. The beheader is here beside me. I hardly need reminding. Clarence deals bluntly, and means my end not in play. In play I played myself into the king's role, giving Polski merriment. It was his death to find me earnest. Now on the same day I must go. All-captivating Clarence consolidates his conquest, taking captive Czars and Kings but dispatching *me* off, his predecessor not remote enough on a throne my buttocks have made hot. I leave him heat: he cools me off.

"Give Clarence credit for killing Polski's former Queen, but first by cheapening her honor; he sent her off compromised, to his own gain of already-owned assets; male vanity, Casanova's endless pride.

"I admit killing Polski himself. At least it wasn't tarnished by a sex act. It was clean and swift. Valorously, I took his place. The place continued slippery, I slide off the diving throne, a murdered murderer too soon.

"It's my pre-death oration, from a former pre-king. Heed me, subjects. I leave behind gold, in abundance. I own property and such real estate that an inflation is threatened. I was titled, before

Poland was mine. Of Aragon I was Duke, and Baron of Cambodia, and Talismania's Treacherer. It's my legacy to the people, to the poor of Poland. May these poor fools inherit such spoils wisely. In return erect a monument to me, immortality's public hint. Concede this, Clarence. It would appease my post-death vanity, and partly pacify my wrath. Do this for old Booboo your former toy. I'm like Falstaff to your becoming Henry the Fifth: we used to roister together, now your dignity disowns me. I'm tragic, and of Falstaff's roundly dimensions. And you're the Prince. What signify those parallels? Death is the gap between correspondences, widening and heightening them.

"Reconsider, Clarence. In charity, lenience, and mercy, can you unsentence me of my unheading as a penalty outside my deserving? Why punish *my* crime? Is not *man* inherently a criminal, as his birth-mark? Spare me, with this consideration. Just grace enough, to carry life over to an extension of its allotment. My arms are bound, and bowed my head. I'll give you tribute, even to retracting my curse on your usurper-usurping soul. Melt and relent, sweet Prince. Forgive. And I will, too."

(There's a touching Scene on stage, Booboo's mercy plea. Is Clarence hard to it? A new Act, to tell that. Clarence looks cold. Disdain grips his voice. A stonely negative reply looks down on the supplicating petitioner for a reluctantly lost life. Booboo kneels in vain. Rejected, he rises in fury. And wild words lash out, his life's last, surging into death:)

"You'll regret not rescinding my sentence."

"My act claims this apology: I'm avenging noble Polski's foul murder, by committing its committer to a similar state. That vindicates my having you quit life. I'm righteous for Poland, which your sacrifice will serve. Your own deed justifies my retaliation; you slew me, a Polish patriot, in slaying my noble King. You're no Pole, nor was your Lady. Yet you infested us. You're both well turned out, return barred; appeasing our grief for our good God, Polski, whom I succeed after your depraved license."

"Hypocrite! You killed his wife, Polski's widow, after carnalizing her in her weak leaving. Rascal, you're unclean yourself, and had led the conspiracy to doom the king you say you loved. You're trying to look good before this crowd. Your crime is still bleeding, and you're the guilty conqueror, guiltier than I whom you vanquish. You cheat your own responsibility: you would whitewash your deed, and perfume its evidence. Your deceit's transparency is the world's most gaped-at gap. You're no priest to absolve yourself, with religious afterthought once your complicity gave instrumental foulness to our low deed. Own you did it, with man's admission, thief! Or would being frank despoil your image of its dandied impunity? You stink high-hell! This is an open verdict for all to see, even the foreign prisoners who dignify our free assemblage as ranking rulers of their threatened lands, landed into your custody on criminal ransom for the nations they lead. This crime is self-doomed in arrogance, and retribution is easily predicted upon you for raping up more than you can chew. You'll pay, quite soon! I bring down this wrath upon you, from your raped victims and the ones you threaten bluster on to subject them to your villainy. Repent suddenly with religion or else let the Furies feast a torment on you, intestinal coils torn out in loops by Harpies of your pillaged women and such ravished soils you contemplate. You go too far against Earth, she'll bounce you back and reflect your handsome face in her blood-muddied pool. Women will rise, and slice you up for scorning them like Orpheus the Greek who ignored them in insolent chastity whereas you put them lustfully to depravity and arrogantly will suffer for it, since Nature doesn't forgive easily. My prophetic curse is on you. Its workings out will slowly crush you down. Too bad I won't witness it. But I've pre-seen it. I was that pre-king, doing pre-seeing upon my princely successor. You'll die soon after me. And much less gloriously."

"I've tolerated too long your idly wicked tongue. I don't dignify it by passing any credit on it. You're mad and sore to be leaving. You wail out, and rent your deranged agony of senses in a seeming sequence of words that fall logically apart. You're not in good order for your going. We'll gag you before extracting your head. Silence becomes a former Monarch."

"Please these final few words. Pardon me, Prince, for blasting you. But there are a few leftover odds and ends that my account needs settling by in balancing my registry and leaving my ledger neat for those to study in their doctoral thesis. Posthumously, it would be too late, to clear these matters up. Grant me such indulgence though impatient for me and Poland to part company and the world be left behind with its living yet to do while I'm out. I'm your rival-nemesis, so your eagerness is understandable to have me and life split without recall. I'm compulsive to itemize some sordid bits of miscellanea. Be big, Prince, as I crave it."

"Hurry, since sunset is coming on, ending our March First as the daylit entry in records of marveled-over history. Soon the torches and lamps must be lit, and the cold dusk howls a wolves' reminder of close forests and dangerous neighbors. Russia might be cross with me for kidnapping its Czar, nor would Catholics appreciate my holding custody their darling Pope, and I fear Germany is angry at its Kaiser being tied up when the news spreads there. His English Majesty, as well, we somewhat abuse, much to the annoyance of the entire British Empire. Diplomats and ambassadors are here confiscated, in our round violation of etiquette among nations.

The French democratic President of that people's republic we've seized as well, and Poland abroad gets an infamous reputation for these broad acts. I'm here answerable. There are crucial matters of state. They press their urgencies in. Hurry, then, Booboo, do your housecleaning to leave your conscience free. What petty trivialities jangle in your fat-soaked skull? Give them your last airing."

(This magnanimous gesture in concession to pre-death Booboo's last living request acquits the Prince well among teeming beholders that include the frail sex in that renowned audience. His charity wins admiration. Follows now the final Act ((Scene the same)) of Booboo as alive. It climaxes this gross, familiar person who rose illegally to steal Poland's crown, spurred on by his round but dead wife. Clarence looks magnificent; in fact is. The executioner looks sinister; as he is. Booboo, bound, looks abject. Frowning, he emits his surly blast to tax his lungs their utmost before pierced when the head toggles to collapse the deputy organs and deflate the vehement empire of which the head was leader. The pre-death song, by the wailing stout man who leaves life a Pole but began it not. In a ball of fire, he goes out fuming.)

"Clarence, you've shown contempt for me. Is that fair, I ask? You're patronizing me, you're a Polish aristocrat by descendancy. I'm only an invader here. I invaded to the top, inveigling all the way. Now you invite me to invade death, for which I had congratulated myself on my slovenly unreadiness. All my business had been *here*, in life. The *world* was where I worked, in my Polish office. Now you unemploy me. Without so much as a by-your-leave of reimbursing pension. I'll be *cut off*, air and all. I'll take so much of me with me, that is, of corporeal substance, my ample girth. I'll leave a lingering spirit, to survey the sorry remains in my pale representation. I'll strew my ghostly ashes here, to ignite and crackle at you. I'll come here haunting about, each night, and your palace guards won't keep me out though I slur the password. A nuisanced sprite, I'll prick at you all day, and goad your dementia . . . But bid the executioner wait. These words can hardly edify you in your arrogant disdain. You suffer me to continue. I'm putting on a show, for the people here collected, subjects and foes of your criminal rule. A little more, please. I'm not through."

"The executioner is trembling to get through with his task. You're ill-bred to keep him so waiting. His profession is being slighted, while you malinger, procrastinate, to work him to a rage. End your stay on earth, with its definite termination. Don't blur the fading borders out, but draw a sharp divider. It's dusk now, and you're holding me up with cowardly dawdling."

"I'm delaying your capping and accomplishment of ambitions *I* set you to. You took over power, and I idolized you. Between my wife and me, I had been working my aspirations, and raised ambition to a series of crescendos from recovered momentum. I had been building, building up, higher, higher—*attained* it, in a bloody coup—only to have it sag, when *you* scooped it up, while the rebound let me flat, and I'm fallen—pushed by you. My fortune is about to conclude. My numerous last-minute appeals have methodically been turned down by that cold machine in you bureaucratically spurning me. My disinheritance is complete, my exile is taken, like Dante from his Florence, or predictably next century Joyce from native Dublin, as my clairvoyance fatally gives prophecy to. So soon, Poland will lose my breath. My capacious lungs will doubly ooze to sag. Let me personally reminisce, just before that event. For setting straight the record, if I may."

"You have so much to regret, as you take leave, that your speech would manufacture more time to carry itself than I can regally afford with affairs to put in order of foreign import. My boundaries might be besieged soon, to warn me off my liberties with these crowned heads that I fail to entertain. Brief, Booboo, only five minutes more, and then bare your head to my brute executioner. Agree to that, and now sum up. What has your life left out, unsaid?"

"I wish to declare—"

"Brevity, please, Booboo—or your wind will be interrupted with a slicing down."

"You're lugubrious, Clarence. It's true that night is overtaking us. My minutes dwindle. A cold corpse I'm about to be. The wind is settling low. Howling wolves bring the forest close. The armed force of Russia might march on us, to rescue their precious Czar and do war to annihilate us. I wish I were here to help in the military emergency that's to ensue. There's only one catch or trouble to that: Clarence won't let me. His will sways; the way is out for me, as I weigh down into death to tip the blind and unjust scale that receives judgement on the new conscript pressed into nether service . . ."

"The seconds drag, Booboo—hasten your puffings, please, or I intervene on your life-loving stalling. Round it up, in swift summary."

"How I wag! My crude old heart is maudlin, in tears already, while the world recedes and the executioner's muscles ripple his arms to bulge my ouster from all that's known. I must hurry. I'm sealed up soon. Clarence is worried. He's inherited a hive of hornets to sting him for his trouble. He'll face economic dissension within, a bubble of domestic turmoil to snap him in the nose: then he faces armed might from abroad. The Polish army, so puny, is surely no match for the combined might of Russia on the attack, the British fleet, and Germany on the flank. He'll be hemmed in, captives and all. His resources will turn slim, and depleted reserves will bare flaws in his defense. His dream will go burst. Women will fawn no longer, on his helpless form. Proud now, soon forlorn. In store accumulates the driving misery—"

(Clarence, abruptly shouting:) "Enough! It's time, executioner. You're on cue, so go ahead. Your mission has been overdue."

(Executioner, alarmed, contrite, shaking, terrified, guilty:) "Your Highness, my blade isn't working. It needs to be mechanically adjusted, a screw in place; it went wrong only now. This is most untimely. Poland's night is upon us, and wolves bring the forest close. In three minutes I'll have it repaired. I submit to being beheaded, on myself voluntarily, if this screws up your hectic schedule. The audience has become restless, their feet aflutter, uttering muttering epithets in a storm of mutiny off in the brewing cloud where hisses hint of thunder. Sorry to spring this on you. The loquacity of Booboo is still not halted, till I fix my instrument of beheading, an instant's mending, pardon my slip. Soon, soon, Prince, I fidget with the tools, show constraint in my agony, I place my bungling life in your overtaxed forbearance, my liege."

(Clarence, writhing but subdued and barely under control:) "Time is tolling close, and the awareness sits uneasy. Booboo is momentarily reprieved. His respite is all too brief, to feel relief. The job is finished, on the instant."

(Executioner, in a surge of anguish and grave humiliation:) "I've blundered further, Sir! A cog is lost, crucial to this machine.

My apology. It's so dark, I can't find it. I tinker away, like an incompetent smith. I vow to repair it. Unfurl a later layer of your dwindling patience from its smouldering sheath, while I set about to perfect this machine to work off Booboo's neck and loose his soul (scrawny by comparison) from that earthy body of his. A tiny fraction of a second, and it'll be back in working order. I'm professionally embarrassed, and hope to live it down, or die it up. Keep your fury in, dear Clarence, that so mounts. You're boiling, behind schedule, as ambition seethes, and the powder keg is set to fuse. Restrain exploding now, or your damaged cause will cripple your majestic scheme of world sovereignty. I keep you waiting guiltily, as Booboo did before. Night has attacked us. Just slightly some more."

(Clarence, flurried in worry, in his ebbing, uncontrollable hope, that drains its route despairingly out:) "This is a sorry accident! You bungle on this high stage! Your agitation shows you earnest, though, as you go about your task to remedy the disaster and mend the life-taker. We're in a flurry of haste. Poland is imperiled, say my informative bones. My greatness is to be tested, on the imminence, on a colossal scale. What perturbs me is not petty. I face enemies aggressing, bent to crusade me out of power that I took only today. Alertness resurges to avail me at the crucible. My plight is in motion, the challenge sets its terms, as danger broods to the increase. I even feel fright.

"Foreign armies are marching, our borders are being sealed off. I boast the greatest prisoners. They're my only weapon, to keep the wolf away.

"Executioner, hurry! Booboo still lives! I want the stage rid of him. He's cluttering the scene, like an unneeded whale on a slender beach. I want him gone. Fix that thing! Ready?"

"It's done, Master. Shall I place Booboo on the block, and snap his neck down?"

"Why not? I ordered it, didn't I?"

"It's done then, Prince. See!?"

(The blade comes whizzing down, but not so swift as that creature of decorum, the curtain, which hates bloody upsets. Booboo is dead, that's plain. The play will limp on, minus the monster.)

(The historic day ends, and the following morning begins the Second of March, and our new Act. The Scene is still Poland, but all *of Poland. Catastrophe is crushing Poland. Clarence is stripped of dreaming. What he wanted won't be given. For him it's terrible. His disaster piles up in an agonizing rush of detail. This report lists its salient points:)*

Russia got wind of what was happening and combined forces with Germany, England, Austria, France, and every other European nation. They wouldn't accept Clarence's bluff. That poser or pretender, that presumptuous fop, had taken the world leaders prisoner, for ransom of the states they led; but the rest of Europe wouldn't fall for it, this bully's ruse whose pompous arrogance had no base in power. Slight Poland was easily crushed, the next morning; and the invaders met no resistance. The Palace was besieged and taken; the Czar was liberated, and the Holy Pope, the Austrian Emperor, the King of England, the President of republican France, the German Kaiser, and their slightly lesser peers. Clarence was in hiding in a crypt in the Palace. His slaughtered dreams lay about him, of total world domination. All the people of Poland had welcomed the liberating foreigners and indeed were helping to hunt down this now-despised Prince, promoted from Captain yesterday. Clarence is cringing in the crypt. His fate can't recover from this blow. His greatness is now a fallen paper from mental water. The substance he had hoped for—was hope, no more. This comedown is not to be received happily, by this proud and recent usurper. This gloom lies thick, his thoughts can't pierce it. His sorrow is swollenly inarticulate. Not a word from him. So we leave him there, with misery to attend. We leave earth, to another atmosphere.

(It's now the Spirit Region, as our new Scene and Act. Lady Boo-boo's ghost has been living there. Her husband's ghost has now joined her. They have so much to discuss! Their transcribed dialogue is given its first earth-recording, in its entirety, as follows:)

"So *there* you are! Been waiting here long, you fishy sack? You've slimmed down, I see. Clarence's soldier took you by storm, and your general death was dealt you by a raping private. Well, here *I* am, too. Clarence had me beheaded. It wasn't pleasant. But the latest news is—the Czar and the other royalty have all been rescued by a combined army and navy from every European country. Clarence is hiding, and Poland has now been taken over by Russia as its 'legal' colony. How the world changes! But we're out of it. How's the weather, 'here'?"

"There *is* no weather, former husband."

"Having rejoined you, aren't we still currently married?"

"Where we are is no respecter of any wedded bond or other custom that went down as a habit of earth. This is a Void where spirits dwell. Your familiar rules can't accompany you, to this place."

"Oh, but I want to haggle with you over old unresolved issues with you, my old arguing partner."

"For form's sake and an empty sense of nostalgia, let's do so, but not expect to solve what are now idle and academic matters. There's no use or hope for sensual improvement here. It would even wither Clarence."

"That's strikingly put, my wife. Let's review our former prospects, from our viewpoints of ironic defeat."

"You're fresher from earth than I am, and so closer to what we were. Looking back, Booboo, what can you regret most?"

"Things didn't go as planned. We were to kill Clarence, before *he* did *us* in. He was in humble straits when we hired his service, yet not sufficiently grateful. We granted to make him court paragon helped by his own good looks, and pay him with heaps of gold for helping us complete the takeover, and reward him with rank as our leading favorite—general and minister—though all the while that schemer was planning to outdo us in our evil by finally taking over on top of our own uprise. We were well taken in, he did us in. Then he beheaded me, a stroke that sent me here."

"Welcome, bungling husband. You only deserved it. What other ranklings have accompanied your beheadedness to this infernal dwelling place for those like us who are bodiless? Your reduction amuses me. Rumble out more of these verbal memoirs."

"My ragings have brought no means of exhaustion. Russia was waiting to trap us. *We* aggressed, and the latest news is, Russia has taken us over. *Germany* will be given a slice of us, too. Poor Poland! From within, *I* was to have consumed it. But it's prey to its old border enemies, and goes as spoils to those mightier. World domination was my ambition, as Booboo the Great. Kidnapping the Czar was the first step. But Clarence cut in, cut me off, and himself now has been forced to 'cut out'. Ruthless ambition doesn't always work. Being here can attest to that, right, dear?"

"Right, old fraud. Go grumble some more. Did you ever make a political mistake, in your lengthy reign?"

"You betray your fishmongering ancestry in uncivil London. Your wicked tongue was critical in your death scene, and *still* you're critical. But you can't haunt me, for *I*'m a ghost, as well. After mercy-killing you, I treated you tenderly, you obese whore! I bade the kingdom mourn *you*, rather than King and Queen Polski, and in my coronation I wore black weeds of mourning in memoriam to you, and was to use the royal 'us' and the royal 'we' in speech, as though you were in the adjoining throne as my crowned queen. See what posthumous respect you were being tendered? But Clarence cut in, to cut short my grief for you, by dishonoring both of us by a beheader's stroke. We're brought together here, in the clash of our discontent spirits in this dismal nether region. Our enmity has pursued us, and resumes here."

"I suggest we make a combined haunting expedition on living Clarence, then, hidden in a crypt, and plague him right to death, or torment him close to it. As a husband-and-wife haunting team we make a fat pair of ghosts, but unseen. Surely you're mad at him and vowed sore revenge when your plea for mercy was dismissed. Here's your chance for treachery, far belated. But before we dive-bomb our former youthful aid, I have a topic to bicker about with you."

"Hateful wench!, What is it?"

"As a Spirit I see clearly into the thoughts of the living. That Private Anonymous who sullied my honor and then battered me almost to death, you were to bring him to justice through an inner-army spy investigation trap. You hoped to send him in your place to appease my wrath that was intended for *you*. My dying vow was to haunt you like a shrew harpy and bitter screeching fury to bewitch you endlessly with shrill perturbances. To placate me from that, you were to send my molester and doer-in as a fit sacrifice, in your own dirty stead. *He* was rough and uncouth, but *you* were a brute, and I would have refused him, so as to torture *you*—but you died instead. You finished me off, remember?, to hasten my approaching death. Now I can't harm your spirit. It frustrates me, your not being alive enough to test what lack of mercy I have. The Private who was to replace you—he turned himself in to claim the reward you were to offer for the apprehension of my rape-killer. He turned self-informer; out of greed, I suppose. What a comic quirk of avarice! The sorry sop! But I liked his body in mine. Jealous? Good. What does it matter now?

"Let me continue. You fume indignation, with your spittly sputterings and phlegm-honking? What an unquiet ghost you are! He was a wild soldier. But his crime is less than yours. Yet I can't punish you, for you're here already. The torture against you, which I'm prohibited to employ, will be visited on Clarence instead, in double fury. Let's go swooping down, and blitz his nerves out, in his hidden crypt, with our otherworldly attack. Quick, before the Russians find him. The *Czar* has designs on him; his cruelty would be great. Let ours be subtle, and swifter."

"You're true to the way you were in real life! Right in your own character! Not a bit changed!"

"No one is. We're the same spirit. But not body-weighted: our only difference, from the foul atmosphere here, to the Polish scene. Let's return there. We'll find the Palace crypt, where squats Clarence, murky, damp, dark, frightful of any footstep. It will be fun, for us. As for the expense, let it be his. *He* can pay. He's still body-chained, and that's what bodies are for: to help mental suffering along, with real pain. Follow me, Booboo, with your new 'wings'. We need no fuel for our raid. It's all free of charge. The *victim* always pays!"

(In glee, Lady Booboo urges her mate like she used to do in life. He's glad, he wants to harangue Clarence, and mock his successor-by-execution, to repay a cruel deed in dissimilar coin. Thus the Scene shifts to earth, and in Poland is our next Act. Spirits will mingle, with the real.)

"Lady Booboo, are you not leading me astray? As ghosts we flutter, and get nowhere. I see no Poland or palace yet, though our flight has taken an age."

"You still haven't sloughed off your worldly 'time' sense. As spirits, we're not in the time *element*. So you can forget it."

"All right, but my chart tells me how due we are in the crypt, only still we're not there. Is impatience the wrong attribute of a ghost?"

"Look, Booboo. On earth, all you ever did was wrong. As a Spirit in time's nether region, or here on our revisiting tour, you're characteristically just as wrong. You never step out of your character: only out of your body."

"All right, bitch. Get me Clarence. Vengeance is smarting. I'm riled, all right. He'll get it, from me!"

"You sound vicious."

"I *feel* it! However carnally null, I'm mentally full. Clarence cost me my life. I'm not kindly disposed, for that reason. And so—
"

"Shut up. As a spirit, you're just wind. Now we alight. Here are the Palace guards, only they're Russian, not ours. There are Cossacks searching for missing Clarence. We'll descend to the crypt. We're there now, and we glide through, to enter the barred door. Here he is!"

(Clarence is spotted, dimly through the murk. He's scared. His tormentors have arrived. He's on his hands and knees: visible. The Booboos are invisible, though both still gross. Their tongues snarl, hiss. High venom from the dead will assault the helpless living quarry. An ugly poison of the mind is being mixed, and served:)

"Clarence, I'm Booboo. Am I heard here?"

(Clarence, quavering:) "Heard, yes. Will you rescue me, or plague me? The real Russians are after me. They're stalking me,

I can't sleep. What are *you* here for, when not resting among the dead? And is that witch-bitch with you? I've come to grief. Is this relief?"

"No. More grief."

"Since that's unwelcome, I bid you leave. And cart your ugly *wife* away, as well. Offensive woman!"

(Lady Booboo:) "Clarence, we refuse to go. And your insult offends me. I'll taunt you, lady-killer! Women always fell for you. Not me, though, being a ghost; I'm immune to your charms. I'll raze you. I'll be brutal. You can't strike me, I have no substance. But my *voice* pierces you!: and you can't slay it!"

(Clarence, wailing, in fright, resigned:) "I'm damned, then!"

(Booboo:) "Yes, but so are we. Your body is an extra pain-giver; we're devoid of that impediment, hence better off, by the pain scale. . . . Well, well. What happened, Clarence? Is *this* greatness?"

(Clarence moans, in his foul dungeon. He groans, in terror. Mercifully drop the curtain, to end the Act. Spare him, by that slight divider.)

(Same Scene, but a new Act. Same lousy crypt. Same ghostly Boo-boo pair. And the trembling Clarence, so brave yesterday, conqueror of Space: today, a rat, in extreme fear. Booboo's haranguing is now launched:)

(Booboo as bully, in the ghostly form:) "All I'm going to do is denounce you, and you can't avoid hearing it, since you dare not leave your hiding place with Russians crawling after you. I gave you a dying vow of curse, should you behead me, which you did: that you'd be dead soon after me, and less gloriously even; that terror would be your bride, to wed forever. Moreover, you ignored my dying request that a monument memorializing me to my undying honor as a glorious patriot and Poland's brief king, be erected. You might claim you didn't have time to order it made, due to pressing pressures from outside. After all, you were soon invaded, surrounded, by nations whose revered leaders were being held illegally in custody by you, a self-proclaimed Prince-thug. You inherited domestic problems as well, from my rule: interior Poland was rife for dissension, and economic distress. Sorry I left you our state in such turmoil. You *took* it, I didn't give it. And *now*, look at you!

"I'm not finished. I willed, remember, all my wealth to the Polish poor. But you would have confiscated it to enrich your princely greed. And after I had sworn allegiance to you! You had won me over, I was ready to obey. I was awed of you, and content to serve you, as slave to idol. You had transformed me from material gold-greed, to Clarence-worshipper. I was to be 'Royal Saint Booboo', as you ordained me, though servile to you. I would *not* have rivalled you, but given deep submission.

"Then you objected to my speech, yesterday afternoon, it seemed to slight or betray you, or be incriminating. So you condemned my head off. And this play would have been minus me as monster: my *ghost* is monstrous, though. It howls at you, with words impossible to oppose, as they issue from no lips. Nor shall yet any silence bless you: my railing has more to go, and then my wife's is next.

"You have a *Russian* foe? They'll seem a *friend*, after *our* voices get through.

"Yesterday you were born as the sun. You were to dominate every universe, and stop not even at infinity's end. You were God's omnipotent rival. You had an emperor's grandiosity to be the human ruler of time and history, in your perpetually youthful dynasty. You were to start with the *Russian* conquest, then annex to your kingdom every immortal realm. March First would be a divine holiday. Your destiny was to incorporate all spiritual life into your greedy worldly ends. You'd go on, and be never stopped. But *should* you come to a halt, it would mean the world's end, history being cut short, the cosmic ruin of heaven itself. Should *you* go, *all* would go. But women would save you. They were your slaves. They'd prevent any lessening in you, and deprive Death of you. All that you figured. Did it come true?"

(Clarence:) "No. But if I had left *you* to rule, your *own* dreams would have been crushed. You were holding European royalty for dirty ransom, and would, like me, have been invaded. It was a mercy for you to die before. Now *I* inherit the disaster. We're thick as thieves, you and I. And the *female* Booboo, that whale of invisibility."

(Madam Booboo:) "Clarence, the end is near. You'll join us among the damned, won't you?"

(Clarence, steadily sober:) "It seems I'm shorn of my ideals. I was so good with women, too! Or bad; it's all the same. I'm trapped in this crypt, and will starve, unless I escape. I'll go out in disguise. No, my face is too known. Unshaved, still it's *my* beard, and my beautiful features. Hope is gone. The Russians want me. The Booboos are plaguing me. The Polskis are both dead. Hell is soon. I'm in its foyer now. Being drawn in to its center. Why did I connect with the Booboos? They brought me down in ruin, by a bad gamble I rode in on and then was to trump. I'm only so young! My virility is so *charged* with a future! Death, then, must be a woman. She pines for me."

(The Booboos have disappeared. That's easy, having been invisible anyway. Their *voices* have gone, now. Outside, the cause is lost. Poland belongs to Russia, and a slice to Germany. Czar and peers are all rescued. Death *is* a woman, just for Clarence, in his special case. His crypt darkens slightly, having been already dim. It's his burial chamber. He reclines on the cobbles. A dark wing of Death comes in: like a woman's leg. Enter the *other* wing, as well. She embraces him. His soul is sucked out. He's fornicated dead. He's gone away, to a neutral spirit region. Are the Booboos in the same one, or a different? This can't be told. Poland is done. Its nineteenth century has become nightmare. The principals are gone. The stage has no more Booboos or their ghosts. Nor Polskis nor Clarence. It's all emptied out. Time squeezes it tight.

What has been happening? What dream entered history? Or what reality has been choking it? Sound and sight are still. What was Poland, is no more. The world outside grows bigger. It crams the stage, as the sides all converge. New images burst forth. There's Booboo and his Madam, fresh, pre-ghosts. And youthful Captain Clarence. What do they plot? Fair Poland is the game. The world's innocence is ready for rape; and experienced corruption to flare and fail, as well. The beginning is renewed. The cycle is back, to the start. Here are Booboo-beasts. And the Clarentian upstart. King Polski, unaware; his Queen all-suspecting, but disbelieved. The lights come on. The Booboos brood. Royal assassination, and the pomp of consequence, to seize the throne. They enlist captivating Clarence. He's a glittering aid. He's indomitable. Where will this conspiracy lead? Its wild course is taken. All fortune follows. The act rises. The fall tumbles. Then dark stillness. Then silence. Then what?)

(This play is done. The characters will be heard from no more.)

*"Père Ubu contemplative" by Franciszka Themerson, sketched for the
1964 production of* King Ubu *at the Stockholm Marionetteatern.
black chalk, 23 x 17 cm
oeuvre catalogue number: D64.37*

Marvin Cohen is the author of many novels, plays, and collections of essays, stories, and poems.

His shorter work has appeared in over 100 magazines and books, including: *Ambit, Antaeus, Assembling, Center Magazine, Cricket Addict's Archive, Essaying Essays, Extensions, Harper's Bazaar, Hudson Review, Monk's Pond, The Nation, National Camp Director's Guide, New Directions in Prose and Poetry, The New York Times, Plays from the New York Shakespeare Festival, The Pushcart Prize, Quarterly Review of Literature, Salmagundi, Sun and Moon, Transatlantic Review, The Village Voice, Vogue (UK)*, and *Wormwood Review*.

His writing ranges from the experimental to fable; from poetry to prose; from internal dialogues to playscripts; from art criticism to cricket fandom; from humour to philosophical essays, and from aesthetics to surrealism (he says "if people say so then it must be true").

His 1980 play *The Don Juan and the Non-Don Juan* was first performed at the New York Shakespeare Festival as part of the *Poets at the Public Series*. Staged readings of the play have featured actors Wallace Shawn, Richard Dreyfuss, Keith Carradine, Jill Eikenberry and Mimi Kennedy.

Born in Brooklyn in 1931, Cohen has described himself as one who has "risen from lower-class background to lower-class foreground." He studied art at Cooper Union but left college to focus on writing, supporting himself with a series of odd jobs, from mink farmer to merchant seaman. He later taught creative writing at various New York colleges, including The New School, the City College of New York and Adelphi University.

For a long time, Marvin Cohen has lived in the Lower East Side, New York City, with his wife Candace.

BLANK PAGE BOOKS

are dedicated to the memory of Royce M. Becker,
who designed Sagging Meniscus books from 2015–2020.

They are:

IVÁN ARGÜELLES
THE BLANK PAGE

JESI BENDER
KINDERKRANKENHAUS

MARVIN COHEN
BOOBOO ROI
THE HARD LIFE OF A STONE, AND OTHER THOUGHTS

GRAHAM GUEST
HENRY'S CHAPEL

JOSHUA KORNREICH
CAVANAUGH
SHAKES BEAR IN THE DARK

STEPHEN MOLES
YOUR DARK MEANING, MOUSE

M.J. NICHOLLS
CONDEMNED TO CYMRU

PAOLO PERGOLA
RESET

BARDSLEY ROSENBRIDGE
SORRY, I BROKE YOUR PROMISE

CHRISTOPHER CARTER SANDERSON
THE SUPPORT VERSES